A WORLD OF LOVE

The Marquis was looking at her once again in that deep, penetrating way.

"I wish you would tell me what is worrying you."

"I cannot think why you should... say that I am ... worried," Carmella replied hesitatingly.

Because what he said made her more frightened than ever that he might guess her secret, Carmella turned away.

She had one foot on the bottom step of the staircase and her hand was on the bannister when the Marquis said:

"If you trust me, you will find me a very good friend."

Just for a moment her eyes were held by his, and she felt as if the Marquis was drawing her with a strange power and magnetism...

Then with a sigh that was almost a cry, she ran away from him up the stairs as quickly as she could.

A Camfield Novel of Love by Barbara Cartland

"Barbara Cartland's novels are all distinguished by their intelligence, good sense, and good nature..."
—ROMANTIC TIMES

"Who could give better advice on how to keep your romance going strong than the world's most famous romance novelist, Barbara Cartland?"
—THE STAR

Camfield Place,
Hatfield
Hertfordshire,
England

Dearest Reader,

Camfield Novels of Love mark a very exciting era of my books with Jove. They have already published nearly two hundred of my titles since they became my first publisher in America, and now all my original paperback romances in the future will be published exclusively by them.

As you already know, Camfield Place in Hertfordshire is my home, which originally existed in 1275, but was rebuilt in 1867 by the grandfather of Beatrix Potter.

It was here in this lovely house, with the best view in the county, that she wrote *The Tale of Peter Rabbit*. Mr. McGregor's garden is exactly as she described it. The door in the wall that the fat little rabbit could not squeeze underneath and the goldfish pool where the white cat sat twitching its tail are still there.

I had Camfield Place blessed when I came here in 1950 and was so happy with my husband until he died, and now with my children and grandchildren, that I know the atmosphere is filled with love and we have all been very lucky.

It is easy here to write of love and I know you will enjoy the Camfield Novels of Love. Their plots are definitely exciting and the covers very romantic. They come to you, like all my books, with love.

Bless you,

CAMFIELD NOVELS OF LOVE
by Barbara Cartland

THE POOR GOVERNESS
WINGED VICTORY
LUCKY IN LOVE
LOVE AND THE MARQUIS
A MIRACLE IN MUSIC
LIGHT OF THE GODS
BRIDE TO A BRIGAND
LOVE COMES WEST
A WITCH'S SPELL
SECRETS
THE STORMS OF LOVE
MOONLIGHT ON THE SPHINX
WHITE LILAC
REVENGE OF THE HEART
THE ISLAND OF LOVE
THERESA AND A TIGER
LOVE IS HEAVEN
MIRACLE FOR A MADONNA
A VERY UNUSUAL WIFE
THE PERIL AND THE PRINCE
ALONE AND AFRAID
TEMPTATION OF A TEACHER
ROYAL PUNISHMENT
THE DEVILISH DECEPTION
PARADISE FOUND
LOVE IS A GAMBLE
A VICTORY FOR LOVE
LOOK WITH LOVE
NEVER FORGET LOVE
HELGA IN HIDING
SAFE AT LAST
HAUNTED
CROWNED WITH LOVE
ESCAPE
THE DEVIL DEFEATED
THE SECRET OF THE MOSQUE
A DREAM IN SPAIN
THE LOVE TRAP
LISTEN TO LOVE
THE GOLDEN CAGE
LOVE CASTS OUT FEAR
A WORLD OF LOVE

Other books by Barbara Cartland

THE ADVENTURER
AGAIN THIS RAPTURE
BARBARA CARTLAND'S BOOK OF BEAUTY AND HEALTH
BLUE HEATHER
BROKEN BARRIERS
THE CAPTIVE HEART
THE COIN OF LOVE
THE COMPLACENT WIFE
COUNT THE STARS
DESIRE OF THE HEART
DESPERATE DEFIANCE
THE DREAM WITHIN
ELIZABETHAN LOVER
THE ENCHANTING EVIL
ESCAPE FROM PASSION
FOR ALL ETERNITY
A GOLDEN GONDOLA
A HAZARD OF HEARTS
A HEART IS BROKEN
THE HIDDEN HEART
THE HORIZONS OF LOVE
IN THE ARMS OF LOVE
THE IRRESISTIBLE BUCK
THE KISS OF PARIS
THE KISS OF THE DEVIL
A KISS OF SILK
THE KNAVE OF HEARTS
THE LEAPING FLAME
A LIGHT TO THE HEART
LIGHTS OF LOVE
THE LITTLE PRETENDER
LOST ENCHANTMENT
LOVE AT FORTY
LOVE FORBIDDEN
LOVE IN HIDING
LOVE IS THE ENEMY
LOVE ME FOREVER
LOVE TO THE RESCUE
LOVE UNDER FIRE
THE MAGIC OF HONEY
METTERNICH THE PASSIONATE DIPLOMAT
MONEY, MAGIC AND MARRIAGE
NO HEART IS FREE
THE ODIOUS DUKE
OPEN WINGS
A RAINBOW TO HEAVEN
THE RELUCTANT BRIDE
THE SCANDALOUS LIFE OF KING CAROL
THE SECRET FEAR
THE SMUGGLED HEART
A SONG OF LOVE
STARS IN MY HEART
STOLEN HALO
SWEET ENCHANTRESS
SWEET PUNISHMENT
THEFT OF A HEART
THE THIEF OF LOVE
THIS TIME IT'S LOVE
TOUCH A STAR
TOWARDS THE STARS
THE UNKNOWN HEART
WE DANCED ALL NIGHT
THE WINGS OF ECSTASY
THE WINGS OF LOVE
WINGS ON MY HEART
WOMAN, THE ENIGMA

A NEW CAMFIELD NOVEL OF LOVE BY

BARBARA CARTLAND

A World of Love

A JOVE BOOK

A WORLD OF LOVE

A Jove Book/published by arrangement with
the author

PRINTING HISTORY
Jove edition/February 1987

All rights reserved.
Copyright © 1987 by Barbara Cartland.
Cover art copyright © 1987 by Barcart Publications (N.A.) N.V.
This book may not be reproduced in whole or in part,
by mimeogrpah or any other means, without permission.
For information address: The Berkley Publishing Group,
200 Madison Avenue, New York, NY 10016.

ISBN: 0-515-08882-X

Jove Books are published by The Berkley Publishing Group,
200 Madison Avenue, New York, NY 10016.
The words "A JOVE BOOK" and the "J" with sunburst
are trademarks belonging to Jove Publications, Inc.

PRINTED IN THE UNITED STATES OF AMERICA

Author's Note

MANY of the people in this novel and the descriptions of their behaviour is authentic.

Lady Brooke's wild infatuation for Lord Charles Beresford was to have widespread repercussions.

In 1889, Lady Beresford opened a letter addressed to her husband in Daisy Brooke's well-known flowing hand. In it Daisy accused Charles of *"infidelity"* because his wife was pregnant!

Furious, Lady Charles placed the letter with her Solicitor and Daisy was notified. Upset and apprehensive, she called at Marlborough House and poured out her woes to the Prince of Wales.

Filled with tears, her beautiful blue eyes were more attractive than ever and the Prince fell head-over-heels in love with her. For years he wrote to her—"My darling little Wifie."

The Countess de Grey's infatuation with Harry Cust caused her to behave in a vindictive fashion which was very harmful. She found in his flat love-letters from the Marchioness of Londonderry and because she was jealous, she sent them to the Marquess.

After this, for thirty years, in fact until he died, the Marquess of Londonderry never spoke to his wife, except in public.

In 1830 Thomas Milner began producing tinplate and sheet iron boxes in Liverpool. As his business grew, he became a manufacturer of prototypes of the modern safe.

In the mid-19th Century, thousands of merchants in Britain and the U.S.A. were keeping their cash in iron safes. These key-lock safes offered slight protection against burglary.

A combination lock, introduced in the U.S.A. in 1862 by Linus Yale, Jr., represented a temporary improvement, but skillful burglars soon learned to manipulate the combinations.

chapter one

1886

CARMELLA was sitting in the small Sitting-Room sewing some lace onto one of her mother's gowns.

She was as near to the window as possible because there was a dismal mist over London, and she longed for the clearness of the sunshine that she had loved in the country.

Every day when she awoke she wished she were back at Bramforde House with the gardens filled with sunshine, the sound of the birds, and the horses waiting for her in the stables.

Sometimes she felt she hated every moment that she had to stay in the narrow street, with its rows of identical houses, and a grey sky overhead, which always seemed to be overcast.

And yet she knew they had come to London for the sake of Gerry, and she had agreed whole-heartedly with her mother that it was what they had to do.

When the fourth Lord Bramforde died and his son Gerald inherited, it was very obvious that they could not afford to stay on in the big house which had been the seat of the Bramfordes since the first Lord was Master of the Horse to George II, and would have to find somewhere else to live.

It was Gerald who had pleaded with his mother that they should go to London.

"All my friends with whom I was at Oxford are having a riotous time," he said, "and I cannot bear to stay here, vegetating amongst the cabbages without even a decent horse to ride."

Lady Bramforde had understood what her son felt.

At the same time, she knew, if she was fair, it was Carmella who should, if there was any money, have a Season in London and make her curtsy, if not to the Queen, then to the beautiful Princess Alexandra of Wales, at a "Drawing-Room," in Buckingham Palace.

Carmella was only just eighteen, while Gerald was nearly twenty-two, and Lady Bramforde felt it was only right that her beloved son, now that he was the fifth Lord Bramforde, should have priority and be able to live, at least for a little while, as a gentleman should.

There were long family consultations, until finally Bramforde House was shut up with only two old servants left to act as caretakers.

They journeyed to London, where Lady Bramforde rented a small house off Eaton Square, and Gerald had bachelor rooms like all his friends in Mayfair.

Carmella had been very unselfish when her mother explained that there was no question of her entering Society as a débutante until Gerald was more settled.

Although she would notify the few friends she had in London and hope Carmella would meet them, it was doubtful if this would ensure her being invited to even one Ball.

"I understand, Mama," Carmella had said. "Of course Gerry must have the right clothes and he can hardly go to his Club without a penny in his pocket."

"I only pray that he will not gamble!" Lady Bramforde said fervently.

At the same time, she agreed with Carmella that Gerald must find his feet before anything could be planned for his sister.

"Do not worry about me," Carmella said bravely. "I am perfectly happy with you, Mama, and I will improve my mind by visiting all the Museums and Art Galleries and, of course, the Tower of London."

Lady Bramforde laughed.

"We will certainly do that, dearest."

Unfortunately, soon after they were settled in London Lady Bramforde became ill.

The Doctor ascribed it to the shock of her husband's death, which had been from an accident, and, in fact, she had not been at all strong for some years.

Keeping up a huge house in the country with only a few servants had proved too much for her.

"What your mother needs is rest," the Doctor said to Carmella, "and if it could be afforded, I would wish her to spend the winter in a warm climate like the South of France. But as I know that is impossible, you must just take care of her and keep her from doing too much."

"I will do my best," Carmella promised.

This meant that since Lady Bramforde was confined mostly to the house, Carmella was, too, but she did not complain.

Of course, when she read the social columns of the newspapers and looked in the magazines which depicted the famous Beauties who surrounded the Prince of Wales, she wished a little wistfully that she had a chance of seeing them.

When her mother felt well enough, they would sometimes go into Rotten Row in the morning, and see the ladies driving in their open Victorias drawn by exceedingly fine horses, and the gentlemen mounted on spirited stallions.

They made Carmella long overwhelmingly for the horses that had been left behind in the country.

Now for the last fortnight Lady Bramforde had not been well enough to leave her bed, and Carmella had been up and down the stairs it seemed a thousand times a day to take her everything she needed and to try to prevent her from attempting to get up.

"I must be downstairs when Gerald comes home," Lady Bramforde said. "There is nothing more boring for a young man than to find women sick in bed."

"Gerald will understand because he loves you, Mama," Carmella replied, but that did not prevent Lady Bramforde from wanting to get up.

"Perhaps she will be well enough to come down tomorrow," Carmella told herself.

She knew it was important that her mother should take things very quietly.

She had a sudden fear that she might slip away as her father had done after his accident.

One day he was laughing and saying he would soon be up and riding round the estate; the next morning they found him dead in bed.

He had a smile on his lips as if, Carmella thought, he had just enjoyed taking a high jump in style.

'If anything happens to Mama,' she thought to herself now, 'I will be alone, and I cannot think what I should do, or who would have me to live with them.'

There were very few relatives in London, although there were a number of cousins with the family name of Forde scattered over different parts of the country.

Carmella could not remember even one of them with whom she had a particular affinity, or who had showed much affection for her father, even though he was the head of the family.

"I suppose it is stupid," she reasoned, "but we have always been so content with ourselves—Papa and Mama, Gerry and me—that we did not trouble about the other Fordes. So they conveniently forgot us."

She was therefore quite certain that if her mother should die, there would be nobody who would really wish to give her a home, and she would have to rely on Gerry, who might in a few years get married.

There was little chance, as things were, of her doing the same.

"I am sorry, darling," her mother had said only a week before she was laid up, "that party we attended this afternoon was so dull for you. I was thinking as I looked round the room that everybody there must be over fifty."

"The old General was very interesting, Mama," Carmella answered.

Lady Bramforde gave a little groan.

"You should not be talking to old Generals, but young Subalterns and charming young men who would make you a suitable husband."

Carmella had laughed.

"I do not expect to find one at the sort of parties we have been to recently."

"That is true enough," Lady Bramforde agreed.

She knew that the parties to which they had been invited had all been given by her own elderly relations who were not in the least fashionable and held small and extremely dull "At Homes" at which one of the guests was always the Vicar.

Or there were even duller dinner-parties, where neither the food nor the conversation could be described as having any quality about it.

"I shall have to do something about you, Carmella," Lady Bramforde said. "Although I would not want you to be conceited, you are growing into a beauty, and it is quite wrong for you to spend your time with your mother and her old friends."

"Do not worry about me," Carmella replied. "I am perfectly happy, Mama, and perhaps when he is more acclimatised to London, Gerry will bring home some of his smart friends."

She knew even as she spoke that it was a forlorn hope, for she had the feeling that her brother was rather ashamed of the small town house they had rented near Eaton Square.

It was certainly a great contrast to where he should really be living, in the huge house in which his father and his ancestors before him had all been of great importance in the County.

Suddenly Carmella had an idea.

"Why do we not go home, Mama? I know we could not live in the big house—that would be impossible and far too much for you. But we could take one of the smaller houses on the estate, or even a cottage!"

She went on beguilingly:

"At least we could enjoy the gardens, although they are overgrown, and of course the Park and the fields in which I could ride."

She thought for a moment that her mother was tempted by the idea, but she quickly said:

"No, Carmella. When I agreed to come to London, I

thought first I should be near Gerald and keep, I hoped, a restraining hand on him so that he did not become too extravagant."

She paused and added rather weakly:

"I determined that once Gerald had found his feet, you shall meet the right sort of people who will entertain you, but that is something we cannot do at the moment."

Carmella was aware that this was because fitting Gerald out in the right sort of clothes from a really smart Tailor had cost what seemed an enormous amount of money.

By this time they had all made sacrifices, especially her mother.

'I do not want to go to parties,' Carmella thought now as she stitched away at the lace, 'I just want to live in the country.'

She thought, because she was prejudiced about London, that the sun never seemed to shine, and there was always a taste of fog in the air or the streets were wet with rain.

"I want to go home," she whispered to herself, then knew she was being selfish.

She had just finished stitching the last row of lace on her mother's gown when the door opened, and she glanced round thinking it was one of the maids, when her brother came in.

She gave a cry of sheer delight and jumped up, her scissors falling from her lap as she exclaimed:

"Gerry! How exciting! I had no idea you were coming home this afternoon."

"I wanted to see you, Mella," Gerald replied, using what had always been his pet name for her, "and I desperately need your help."

"My help?" Carmella exclaimed, then questioned: "What has . . . happened?"

She knew by the expression on her brother's face that something was very wrong.

He walked across the room and she could tell by the way he was moving that he was agitated.

As he stood in front of the small fireplace she thought how tall and handsome he looked, and in the smallness of the room, which was not very well furnished, like someone from a different world, which in fact he was.

She moved towards him and putting her hands on his shoulders, kissed his cheek before she said:

"Tell me what is wrong. Mama is asleep, so we shall not disturb her."

"Thank God for that," Gerald said, "because Mama must not know what has happened!"

"What *has* happened?" Carmella asked.

She sat down on the sofa as she spoke, clasping her hands together in her lap and looked up at her brother.

He took a deep breath before he said:

"I have lost a thousand pounds!"

Carmella gave a little gasp before she exclaimed:

"A thousand pounds! Oh, Gerry, how could you? Was it gambling?"

"Yes, gambling," Gerald replied. "I was insane!"

Carmella felt her hands trembling with shock, but she managed to say in her quiet, gentle voice:

"Tell me about it."

For a moment it was difficult for her brother to speak. Then he said:

"My only excuse, and it is not a very good one, is

that I was 'foxed,' definitely 'foxed,' to the point where I was not responsible for my actions, although that would not prevent me from being convicted by any reputable jury."

Carmella gave a cry of horror.

"What do you mean? You cannot mean to tell me that you have done anything... criminal?"

"No, of course not," Gerald said quickly, "not from an official point of view. But from yours and Mama's, it is a crime for which I ought to be hanged on the gallows, or shot at dawn!"

"Tell me... exactly what has... happened."

"You will remember two or three days ago," Gerald said, "Mama gave me her sapphire necklace, our *famous* necklace, to have the clasp mended?"

He said the word "famous" with a sarcastic note in his voice which Carmella knew was because of the history associated with it.

The one thing Lady Bramforde possessed that was of any great value was what was known as the "Bramforde Necklace" which her husband had inherited from his grandfather.

He had left it to her in his will unconditionally, but with the request that she should on her death leave it to Gerald for his son.

Because Lord Bramforde had been so hard up, it was the only thing he could leave his wife, except for a small annuity which would save her from being absolutely poverty-stricken, unless their fortunes turned and Gerald in some way or another managed to make the estate pay.

As this was unlikely, Lady Bramforde had put the sapphire necklace, which was very magnificent to look at, in the Bank, and had forgotten about it.

When however they were searching desperately for money with which to come to London, to set Gerald up as a young Gentleman of Fashion, and also to provide pensions for several servants who were far too old to find alternative employment when they closed Bramforde House, Lady Bramforde had the idea that she must sell the necklace.

"You cannot do that, Mama," Gerry had said quickly. "It will proclaim to the whole world that we are 'below hatches.' Everybody knows that we own the Bramforde Necklace, and it has in fact been described and illustrated in various magazines."

This was because there was a history attached to it. It had been given to the first Lord Bramforde by a Maharajah in India because he had saved his life and it was therefore considered very lucky.

Because Queen Victoria was interested in India, and had been declared Empress in 1876, the story of the Bramforde Necklace had been revived by journalists and made to sound even more exotic and exciting than it was.

It was then that Carmella had an idea.

"Of course you cannot sell it, Mama, as it is. There would be far too much talk and we might even be accused of being unpatriotic."

She paused and went on.

"But why do you not have it copied and sell the original stones separately, which although Papa said many of them were not perfect, would be bound to fetch a considerable sum on money."

At first Gerry had demurred.

Then, because there was no other means of his getting everything he wanted and of providing for the pensioners anything but a pittance, he capitulated.

They had taken the necklace to a trustworthy Jeweller in Hatton Garden, who had copied the sapphires exactly.

As Carmella said, when her mother wore it round her neck, no one could put the stones under a microscope to see if they were the original sapphires or merely glass.

Then the other day, when Lady Bramforde was thinking that as soon as she was well enough, she would take Carmella to some evening parties, she looked at the fake necklace and discovered that the clasp was broken.

"We must have it repaired," she said.

She asked Gerald when he came to see her if he would take it to their Jeweller in Hatton Garden, knowing she dared not show it to anyone less trustworthy than he had proved himself to be.

"I had forgotten about the necklace," Gerry said now, "but then I remembered I put it loose in my pocket, intending to go straight to Hatton Garden before the shops closed."

"And what happened?" Carmella asked.

"I had a message for somebody at White's," Gerry said, "so I stopped there on the way and found a number of friends were celebrating the engagement of Tony Winter to a very beautiful young woman who is also an heiress."

"Who is Tony Winter?"

"He is the elder son of the Earl of Moriton," Gerald replied, "but that is not important! What happened was that first I started to drink Tony's health, then he insisted that he stood us all dinner, and of course we went on drinking."

Carmella drew in her breath, realising what a mistake it had been, but she did not say anything, and her brother continued:

"When I had drunk considerably more than was good for me, we went into the Card Room to see what was going on there. We started to gamble amongst ourselves, making rather a joke of it. It was then that Ingleton came in, and seeing there was no play at the other tables, he joined ours."

"Who is Ingleton?" Carmella asked.

"Good Heavens! Do you never read the newspapers?" Gerry enquired. "The Marquis of Ingleton is, I suppose, the most talked-of man in Society!"

He stopped, then went on impressively.

"He is not only a friend of the Prince of Wales, but he owns the best race-horses, which invariably are first past the winning-post, he is enormously rich, and they say that every woman he meets throws herself into his arms."

Carmella gave a gasp at the way he spoke, and Gerry went on:

"Personally I loathe him! He is stuck up and supercilious! He behaves as if he owns the world, while everyone else walking on it is less than the dust."

"But you . . . played with . . . him," Carmella said in a very small voice.

"I must have been mad—crazy! No, the truth is, I was drunk! 'Drunk as a Lord!' as they say, and in my case very appropriately!"

"What happened?"

"Need you ask?" Gerry said. "The others very wisely, after a few hands, pulled out of the game, and I was left alone confronting the Marquis. Because I dislike him, I would not let him be the victor, which he was quite sure he was going to be."

He walked across the small room and back again before he said:

"We got down to the last two cards, and the Marquis, without even turning his up, said:

"'I will wager this!'

"As he spoke he pushed forward his winnings and the money he had put down on the table when he arrived. It was a huge pile of gold, and I thought it was an added insult that he had not even bothered to look at the card he held, he was so damnably sure that he could defeat me."

Carmella made a little murmur of sympathy, and her brother continued:

"I put my hand into my pocket and found it was empty. Then instead of capitulating, as anyone except a fool would have done, I felt in my other pocket and my fingers encountered Mama's necklace."

"Oh, no!" Carmella breathed, guessing what had happened next.

"I told you I was 'foxed,'" Gerry said, "and I flung it down on the table and said: 'And I wager that against you, My Lord!'

"I heard somebody murmur: 'The Bramforde Necklace. They say it is very lucky!'"

"Then what happened?" Carmella asked in a whisper, knowing the answer.

"The Marquis said, drawling the words:

"'Seeing what you are staking, Bramforde, I suggest you turn up your card first.'"

Gerald drew in his breath.

"Even then I was still defiant, thinking perhaps at the

back of my mind that the necklace really was lucky. I turned over my card."

"What... was it?"

"The Six of Clubs."

"And the Marquis's?"

"There was a perceptible pause, as if he deliberately made me suffer by waiting," Gerald said angrily. "Then slowly, with that look of contempt on his face that made me long to strike him, he turned up his card, and it was the King of Hearts!"

Carmella gave a cry.

"Oh, Gerry, how could you do anything so crazy?"

"That is what I have been asking myself ever since," he said. "I suppose I must have looked a bit knocked out, because the Marquis picked up the necklace and put it in his pocket. Then he said:

"'As it is difficult to assess the value of anything so historic, I suggest, Bramforde, we make it a round sum of one thousand guineas with the usual month to pay. Do you agree?'

"It was difficult, but I managed to reply: 'Certainly My Lord,' and walked away."

There was silence. Then Carmella said in a voice that was a little incoherent:

"H-how can you... find a thousand pounds in a... month? It is impossible!"

"It is not the thousand pounds that matters so much," Gerald said, "it is the fact that if I do not pay, Ingleton will soon learn that the necklace is a fake."

"I had forgotten that!" Carmella exclaimed. "He must never know! If he does, he will talk and people will say terrible things about Mama for selling the original stones."

"Of course they will!" Gerald agreed. "That is why we have to prevent it at all costs."

"But... how can we f-find a thousand pounds? Will anyone buy anything we possess."

"We have been through that before," Gerald replied. "You know as well as I do that the House is entailed onto the son I shall never have. So is the Estate which I cannot afford to farm."

"Then what can we do?" Carmella whispered.

"What I am going to do," Gerry said, "with your help, is to steal back the necklace."

"Steal it?"

Carmella's voice rose to a cry.

"Yes, steal it," he replied.

"B-but... how? I... I do not understand what you are... s-saying."

"After I left the Card Room I heard one of my friends say to the Marquis: 'What are you going to do with the famous necklace, My Lord? You know there are a lot of thieves about.'

"'I am aware of that,' the Marquis replied. 'I am going to the country tomorrow, and I shall take it with me and put it with the Ingleton jewels in a safe which, I assure you, is burglar-proof!'

"There was laughter at this, then the Marquis left the Card Room and I went downstairs to the Bar to have a drink which I felt I needed because I was beginning to realise what I had done."

Carmella thought it was a mistake for him to have continued drinking, but she did not say so and Gerald went on:

"Sir Robert Knowsbury, an old friend of Papa's who has always been very kind to me, came up and said:

'What have you been up to, Gerald? You look a bit "white round the gills."'

"'I am, Sir Robert,' I replied.

"'You must tell me about it,' Sir Robert said, and at that moment the Marquis joined us.

"'I have been looking for you, Knowsbury,' he said. 'I am giving a party next weekend at Ingleton, and I would like you to come.'

"'That is very kind of you,' Sir Robert replied.

"'Bring Lady Isabel with you,' the Marquis went on. 'I have already invited her, and I know she would like you to drive her down.'

"'That is something I shall be delighted to do,' Sir Robert replied.

"The Marquis was just about to walk away," Gerry continued, "when he looked at me and said:

"'Your luck was not in tonight, Bramforde, and I feel you should have a chance to win back your losses. Suppose you stay with me next weekend?'

"I was so taken aback," Gerry said, "that without even thinking, I stammered: 'Thank you, My Lord.'

"'Perhaps, as you will not know many of my guests,' the Marquis said, as if he had suddenly thought of it, 'you could bring a friend along. But make it somebody beautiful and, of course, sophisticated. Sir Robert will tell you what my parties are like.'

"Before I could reply he had walked away."

"And you had accepted to stay with him?" Carmella asked.

"It was only later when my friends came downstairs that I learnt that was where the necklace would be," Gerry replied. "So it is essential that we should go to Ingleton Hall. . . ."

"We?" Carmella interrupted.

"That is where you have to help me," Gerry said simply. "I asked Sir Robert, as the Marquis had told me to do, what his parties are like, and he said:

"'You are a very fortunate young man! Ingleton rarely invites anyone new to his parties, which invariably consist of his very special friends. He also invites the most beautiful women in England and they are usually the Professional Beauties.'"

As if he felt his sister did not understand, Gerald explained:

"The Professional Beauties, as you must be aware, are the women in 'the Marlborough House Set' who are so beautiful that the public stand on seats in the Park to watch them go by, and whose picture-postcards are sold in most Stationers shops."

Carmella was in fact aware of this, and she knew the Countess de Grey was one of the Professional Beauties, as were the Duchess of Manchester, the Countess of Dudley, and Lady Brooke.

"But Gerry, I am sure you know no one like that," Carmella said.

"Of course I do not. I have not even met them!" Gerry replied. "So that is why you have to come with me."

Carmella laughed.

"You must be mad! I am not a Professional Beauty, nor am I in the least sophisticated, and *The Ladies Journal* tells me they are all witty conversationalists."

"You have got to come with me," Gerry said stubbornly. "There is no one else I can take, and no one else I can trust to steal the necklace."

"How can I possibly steal a necklace that is in the family safe?"

"We will have to think of a way," he replied. "Perhaps you could charm the Curator, or whoever it is that looks after the jewels, to show them to you, then sneak it when he is not looking."

Carmella gave a cry of horror.

"Of course I could not do such a thing! If I were caught, I would go to prison, and we cannot humiliate ourselves by becoming common or garden felons."

"All right! You find me a thousand pounds within the next month!"

"We both know that is impossible, and you will have to tell the Marquis so."

"In that case, of course, he will try to sell the necklace, or perhaps first have it valued. Mama will be held up to ridicule, and perhaps even accused by the Forde family of deception."

There was a pause before he went on bitterly:

"After that I shall never be able to hold up my head again. I will have to leave London and live in the country, where no one will see me."

Because Carmella knew what this would mean to him, she rose from the sofa and walked across to the window to stand looking out onto the grey street outside.

The sky above seemed as dark as the darkness which covered her mind and her heart.

How could this have happened? How could Gerry have done anything so insane as to stake and lose the fake necklace? As long as it was not in their keeping, it was like a sword of Damocles hanging over their heads.

"We cannot steal it, we cannot do anything so wrong and wicked," she told herself.

Then she heard Gerry say pleadingly:

"Help me, Mella, for God's sake, help me! Otherwise I had better put a bullet through my head!"

She turned round and it was not the smart, fashionable Lord Bramforde who was looking at her, but a little boy near to tears who had got into trouble with his father, or was desperately unhappy at having to return to School and leaving his family behind.

Impulsively she moved towards her brother and slipped her arm through his.

"I will help you, Gerry," she said, "you know I will help you, but it is going to be very difficult, and not for one moment will the Marquis of Ingleton think that I am a fashionable, sophisticated Beauty."

Gerry looked at her and he said:

"You are beautiful all right, and you have just to get yourself into the part. I do not suppose that in that sort of society anyone will pay very much attention to us anyway."

He dropped his tone as he continued:

"If only we can steal the necklace away from the Marquis, then I can ask him for extra time in which to pay him what I owe him. Unless, of course, as I hope will happen, he will be so overcome at having lost the necklace that he will cancel my debt."

Carmella knew that was reasonable, even though she disapproved.

The whole idea was so frightening that she could hardly contemplate without shuddering, doing anything so disgraceful.

"Promise me one thing," she said quickly, "that you will try to raise the money before you resort to stealing. Surely some of your friends would lend it to you?"

"Most of them are as hard-up as I am," Gerry replied, "and even if they all contributed, I doubt if we would have a thousand pounds by next weekend."

He moved away from Carmella and said:

"I have made a damned fool of myself, and perhaps the best thing I can do is to go abroad—disappear. That would make it uncomfortable for you and Mama, and even if you pleaded with the Marquis to keep silent about it, he would still be aware that the necklace is false."

"Anyway, you cannot do anything like that," Carmella said, "and I suppose we can only try to get it back. Then, if we fail, we shall have to take more desperate steps."

As she spoke she had no idea what they could be, and was quite certain that even if they sold everything they possessed, including their clothes, they would not fetch more than a few hundred pounds.

Every penny they had got for the sapphires of the necklace had been disposed of in one way or another.

Except for a small sum in the Bank which would have to keep them until after the harvest, when they might obtain some rents from the farmers to whom they had let part of the Bramforde Estate.

She doubted if even that would be very much, and although there was some furniture left behind in the Big House, it was entailed onto Gerry.

They had one Trustee, a Solicitor, appointed by her father, who had an uncomfortable habit of checking the Inventory every six months or so.

"Just in case," he used to say, "the servants have stolen something."

Carmella could not help thinking that it was not the servants he suspected of disposing of anything that was entailed, but Gerry himself.

"What can we do? What can we do?" she asked, and felt the question turning over and over in her mind.

As if he were sure there would be no more argument about her acceptance of the Marquis's invitation, Gerry said:

"Now, what you have to do, Mella, is to find some clothes that are smart and sophisticated."

"How am I to do that?" she asked in a frightened voice.

"Well, I think I might be able to help you."

"How ... could you?"

"Well, I have a friend, you do not know him, but he is a very good friend of mine, who is looking after an attractive young woman who is on the stage."

"What do you mean ... he is 'looking after her'?" Carmella asked.

Gerry hesitated before he replied:

"He has known her for some time, and she has not many friends in London."

"Oh, I ... see."

"I believe we might be able to borrow some of her clothes for you."

Carmella stiffened.

"I do not think Mama would like me to borrow clothes from a stranger!"

"Oh, for Heaven's sake!" Gerry exclaimed. "She is a very nice, pretty woman, and exceedingly smart. It is no use saying you will help me if you are going to make objections."

"No ... no ... of course not! No one must know what we did to the necklace, and of course I will help you, dearest, and I am sorry if I am being difficult. It is just that this whole idea frightens me!"

"It frightens me, if you want the truth," Gerry replied, "and the Marquis has always done that."

"Why should you be frightened of him?" Carmella asked. "After all, he is only a man."

"All I can say is, he is not like other men!" Gerry said angrily. "I hate him! I hate the idea of accepting his hospitality, but it is something, Mella, that has to be done."

He looked at his sister and once again she knew he was pleading for help.

"I am sorry," he said. "I know I have made a fool of myself, but I am in the devil of a fix, and I really have no idea how I can get out of it."

Because she loved him, Carmella could not resist the pathetic way he spoke.

She put her arms round his neck and held him tight.

"Do not worry, dearest," she said. "I am sure that somehow, together, we will find a solution, and what I shall do is pray very hard that perhaps Papa, wherever he is, will help us."

chapter two

As soon as Gerald was satisfied that his sister had agreed to everything, he left.

"You must see Mama first," Carmella had said.

"I think that would be a mistake," Gerald replied. "She might think it strange that I have dropped in without some reason, and, quite frankly, Mella, we have to work quickly if you are to look anything like a Professional Beauty by next weekend."

Carmella laughed at this because it was a ridiculous idea, but she understood what her brother was saying and waved him goodbye as he drove off in a smart Chaise he had borrowed from one of his friends.

It seemed extraordinary to her that, if he had a friend who had anything so expensive as a Chaise with two outstanding horses, and another who "looked after," whatever that might mean, a very talented actress, he could not borrow some money from them.

She was aware, of course, it would be very embarrassing and they would not be paid back at all quickly.

At the same time, she was terrified by Gerald's idea that they must steal the necklace and that she had to pretend to be someone smart and sophisticated, which was the last thing she felt.

"Surely," she had said, "the Marquis, knowing you, will expect your sister to be someone quite young and ordinary like me?"

"You are not going to Ingleton Hall as my sister," Gerald replied.

Carmella just stared at him in astonishment, and he explained:

"At these parties, according to Sir Robert, everybody is paired off with somebody they particularly fancy, and to make yourself credible, you will have to pretend to be a lady with whom I am in love."

Carmella gave a cry of horror. Then she said:

"I have never heard of anything so ridiculous! How could the Marquis believe for a moment that you are in love with somebody like me?"

"But you will not look like you," Gerald explained in a pains-taking manner, as if talking to a child. "You have to look like the Beauties you read about in the magazines, and whom, if you would take the trouble to go there, you can see in the park, especially in Rotten Row."

"I have seen them! I have seen them with Mama!" Carmella replied. "And they look unreal, like exquisite flowers, when they are sitting in a Victoria, glittering with jewels and holding tiny sunshades over their heads."

"If you have seen them, then it cannot be too difficult for you to imitate them," Gerald said, "but I will get someone to bring you up to scratch, and the sooner we get on with it, the better!"

He then hurried away, leaving Carmella bewildered, but also aware that she had to help him, however difficult it might seem.

"How can I refuse, Papa?" she asked her father in her heart. "Gerald must not disgrace our name or his position as head of the family now that you are dead."

When she was alone, the full realisation swept over her of how degrading it would be if the whole story came out.

Not only would Gerald be held up to ridicule for having given anyone as important as the Marquis of Ingleton a false necklace, but her mother might be accused of deliberate fraud in pretending that pieces of glass were the original sapphires.

It all seemed so terrifying to Carmella that there was nothing she could do but pray.

She thought that only her father, whom she had always adored, could possibly help them because no one on earth would be likely to do so.

"Help us, Papa, help us!" she said silently over and over again.

It seemed like an answer to her prayer when later that day, after she had tucked her mother up for the night and left her to sleep peacefully, a maid had come to her room to say there was a messenger at the door with a letter for her.

Because they could afford only cheap and not very well-trained servants, the maid, who was quite young, had difficulty in explaining who was there.

Carmella went down the stairs to find standing at the front door a man wearing the livery of one of the Clubs to which Gerald belonged.

"Are you Miss Carmella Forde?" he asked.

"I am," Carmella confirmed.

"I've a note, Miss, from Lord Bramforde," the man said. "'E tells me to give it into your own 'ands, and not leave it with anyone else."

"I understand," Carmella replied, "and thank you very much! It is very kind of you to bring it."

She took the letter, then hesitated and said:

"Will you wait for a moment while I give you something for your trouble?"

She knew this was the correct thing for her to do, but the man smiled, touched his cap, and said:

"That's all right, Miss. His Lordship's already looked after me."

He walked away, and Carmella was left with the note in her hand.

She shut the front-door and went into the Sitting-Room feeling apprehensive at what Gerald had to say to her.

She opened the envelope and found it was a very brief letter.

She read:

Dearest Mella,

Everything is all right, and Mademoiselle Yvonne Foublane says she will be delighted to help you. I will pick you up at two o'clock tomorrow afternoon. You had better tell Mama I am taking you for a drive in the Park.

I am sorry I have made such a fool of myself.

Love,

Gerry.

Because he had apologised, Carmella felt the tears come into her eyes.

She wondered what Mademoiselle Yvonne was like, and how Gerry had persuaded her to help them.

She found it impossible to sleep, but lay awake, thinking how terrible it was, after all the trouble her mother had taken to raise enough money to make it possible for Gerald to be in London with his smart friends, that they were now in such dire straits.

"A thousand pounds!"

The words seemed to repeat and repeat themselves over and over in her mind.

She felt they were written on the darkness, and she could see a thousand golden sovereigns twisting away like a snake into an indefinable distance.

When Carmella awoke, the words were still there pressing on her brain insistently and inescapably.

With them was the mental picture she had of the Marquis as Gerry had described him.

Cold, cruel, cynical, sarcastic, and waiting, she was sure, to punish Gerry if he found out that he had deceived him.

She spent the morning, when she was not with her mother, staring at herself in the mirror and trying to arrange her hair in a more sophisticated manner.

It seemed to her that everything she did only made her look younger and more countrified than before.

"It is hopeless, quite hopeless!" she told herself. "I cannot think why Gerry cannot persuade *Mademoiselle* Yvonne to go with him."

She said the same thing to her brother when he came to collect her at two o'clock again in a borrowed Chaise, much smarter than anything he could afford himself.

Carmella sat beside him and she was sure that if they kept their voices low, the groom, who was sitting perched on the small seat behind them, could not overhear what was said.

"I think it is hopeless to try to alter me," she told

him. "I wonder why you do not ask *Mademoiselle* Yvonne to go with you."

"You must be crazy," Gerald replied. "The Marquis would not invite that sort of woman to one of his parties."

As Carmella gave a little gasp, he said quickly:

"I mean, because she is an actress, she would not fit in with the smart ladies he entertains."

"But she is willing to help me?"

"As I told you, she is looked after by my friend the Viscount Turnleigh, and as he is in the country with his parents at the moment, I spend quite a lot of time with her."

This seemed to Carmella understandable, but when she met *Mademoiselle* Yvonne, she was astonished both at her appearance and the familiar way in which she talked to Gerry.

Mademoiselle Yvonne's house, which Gerry had explained belonged to the Viscount, was in St. John's Wood, an attractive-looking residence with a small "in and out" drive in front of it, where it was convenient to leave the Chaise.

A smart maid-servant in a frilly lace apron and cap to match opened the door.

She curtsied and said:

"Nice to see you, M'Lord. *M'mselle*'s waiting for Your Lordship in her bedroom."

Carmella thought this was rather strange, but she said nothing, and was impressed by the thickness of the carpet on the stairs and that the walls were decorated with a bright and rather pretty wallpaper.

When they entered *Mademoiselle*'s bedroom, which was on the First Floor, Carmella had great difficulty in not giving an audible gasp of astonishment.

The room seemed to be entirely dominated by an enormous double bed hung first with frilled white muslin curtains from a gold corolla on the ceiling, then over them curtains of silk which were of a vivid blue that was echoed by the carpet.

The curtains over the window were in contrast a brilliant coral pink with masses of tassels and were braided and draped in a manner that Carmella had never seen before.

But as she entered she had eyes only for *Mademoiselle* herself, who was lying back against a number of silk pillows edged with lace and wearing, as Carmella recognised, what was known as a negligee.

In contrast again to the rest of the room, it was emerald green and trimmed with lace besides velvet ribbons of the same colour, and when she moved it was almost transparent.

Her dark hair was falling over her shoulders and she sprang up as Gerry appeared and ran across the room, to Carmella's astonishment, to fling her arms around his neck.

Carmella was certain that she wore little or nothing beneath her negligee.

Mademoiselle kissed Gerald on both cheeks, exclaiming as she did so:

"*Bonjour, Monsieur* Milord! I am very 'appy to see you and you 'ave brought your sister to meet me which ees a verry great pleasure."

She took her arms from around Gerald's neck as she spoke and held out her hand to Carmella, saying as she did so:

"*Mon Dieu*, but you are so pretty—*non!* Beautiful

ees the right word, and it ess a pity that we 'ave to—'ow you say?—'gild the lily!'"

Carmella realised she was being very pleasant.

At the same time, it was difficult not to stare at *Mademoiselle*'s large eyes, with her eye-lashes heavily mascaraed, and her attractive curved lips to which she had undoubtedly applied a great deal of lip salve.

She was not beautiful, or even pretty, but Carmella realised she had a fascination that she had never seen before.

Her eyes slanted up a little at the corners, her face was a perfect oval, and although her skin was not as white as it was fashionable to be, there was no doubt that rouge and powder contributed to the fact that she was arrestingly alluring.

"And now, Yvonne," Gerald said, "I have brought my sister Carmella here, because we need your help and you know as well as I do how fastidious the Marquis is."

Mademoiselle Yvonne laughed.

"Eef you 'ope your sister weel fascinate that 'Mountain of Ice,' you are wasteeng your time! When 'e seets in the Royal Box, lookeeng with those disdainful eyes, the whole Theatre goes cold! I am glad for the moment I do not 'ave to see them, and I am very 'appy just acting for Milor."

Gerry coughed and said quickly:

"My sister knows you are on the stage, Yvonne, and that is why you will be able to help her act the part of a sophisticated Beauty for the two days we have been invited to Ingleton Hall."

Mademoiselle did not speak, and he went on with a warning glance at Carmella:

"As I have explained to you, I made a bet, and quite a large one, that I will take somebody to Ingleton Hall who is quite different from his usual lady-guests, and the Marquis will not have the slightest idea of it."

"*Oui, oui,* you told me," *Mademoiselle* Yvonne said, "and I thought you would 'ave no chance of winneeng, and the Marquis would discover your masquerade *immediatement,* but now I am not so sure."

She stood looking at Carmella as she spoke, moving a little from side to side with one hand on her hip.

As one of the windows was behind her Carmella tried not to be shocked when she saw *Mademoiselle*'s figure outlined against the sunshine.

"*Tiens!*" *Mademoiselle* said after a long inspection. "What you ask me ees deeficult, but not *impossible.*"

"Good for you!" Gerry exclaimed. "I knew you would not fail me."

"Eet weel not be easy," *Mademoiselle* Yvonne replied reprovingly. "Your sister is—'ow do you say?—like a beauteeful Eenglish rose. To turn 'er into an exotic orchid will require a magic wand!"

"Which I am sure you have," Gerry said, "and you know, Yvonne, that I shall be very, very grateful."

"As you told me last night," Yvonne replied.

She gave him what Carmella thought was a mischievous look from under her long eye-lashes.

Then Gerry looked embarrassed and said:

"I think it would be best if I wait downstairs while Carmella tries on the clothes you have in mind for her."

"That ees a good idea!" *Mademoiselle* Yvonne agreed. "Sit comfortably, and read ze boring Engleesh *Times* which Tony 'as delivered every day, and ask ze servants to bring you bottle of 'is best champagne!"

"I will certainly do that!" Gerry replied with a grin. "And do not frighten Carmella. She has never met anyone like you before."

"*La, la,* I understand that," *Mademoiselle* Yvonne replied, "and you know well she should not be meeting me now, but in emergency it is—'ow do you say?—all 'ands to ze pump!"

Gerald laughed, then as he left the room *Mademoiselle* Yvonne said:

"Now we get busy. Take off your bonnet, *Mademoiselle,* and I call my maid to 'elp you."

She rang the bell and when a middle-aged woman dressed in black appeared, she started to speak to her very rapidly in French.

Carmella was quite fluent in French because her mother had insisted that every educated lady spoke French.

She understood that *Mademoiselle* was asking for gowns that were smart without being theatrical, sophisticated but not outrageous.

"*Oui, M'mselle, je comprends,*" the maid said, and added: "It is by good fortune that *l'Anglaise* is about the same size as yourself."

"That is what Milord said," *Mademoiselle* laughed, "and who should know better than he?"

The elderly maid disappeared, and Carmella, having taken off her hat, stood bewildered in the strange room, thinking she had never imagined that Gerry could know anyone like *Mademoiselle* Yvonne or be so familiar with her.

The maid came back with an armful of clothes, and as she helped Carmella out of her gown, *Mademoiselle* Yvonne spoke.

"Eef you intend on deceiving ze Marquis so that your brother can win 'ees bet, you weel 'ave to be very clever."

"I am very frightened in case I fail him."

"I love your brother, 'e ees a verry nice man, verry kind. Eer ees a pity because 'e so poor 'e cannot..."

As if *Mademoiselle* Yvonne realised she was about to say something very indiscreet, she stopped and pointed out to her maid, who was called Jeanne, that the gown into which she had just helped Carmella was a little too loose in the waist.

"Eef you really 'ave a smaller waist than I, *Mademoiselle*, I shall be verry, verry jealous. Mine ees seventeen and a half. What ees yours?"

"I...I am afraid I do not know," Carmella answered. "I have never thought of measuring it."

"Then you are different from most ladies, who measure their waist every day, and pull their corsets so tight they cannot breathe!"

Carmella laughed.

"That sounds a very stupid thing to do!"

"They wish to be fashionable, and beauteeful," *Mademoiselle* Yvonne said.

The next gown she tried on was too small, and when, to Carmella's embarrassment, *Mademoiselle* made her take off the very light corset she was wearing and replace it with a small one in black lace which she said had come from Paris, Jeanne pulled on the laces at the back until Carmella protested.

"Now you look fashionable," Yvonne said, "and you will see that my gown weel make you look as you weesh, verry sophisticated!"

It certainly gave her, Carmella thought, a figure she

had never had before, and although the smallness of her waist seemed to make her small breasts very prominent, she did not say anything in case it should seem rude.

She tried on three day-gowns, all of which she thought were extremely beautiful, but very much more elaborate than anything her mother would have worn. Although she was afraid to say so, she felt they were over-dressed for the country.

But *Mademoiselle* Yvonne insisted they were just right for her part and then the evening-gowns were produced.

They were fantastic, and again had very tight waists and what Carmella thought was an extremely immodest *décolletage*.

She was sure her mother would be shocked and horrified at her appearance in anything so inappropriate for someone of her age.

"That ees better!" *Mademoiselle* Yvonne said when Carmella was encased in a gown of pink silk trimmed with tulle flounces of the same colour, and tulle sparkling with sequins enveloped her shoulders.

She then made Carmella sit down in front of the dressing-table while Jeanne arranged her hair in a fashion different from any style she had worn before.

It was swept up in the front, which gave her height, and seemed to accentuate the largeness of her eyes and her small classical features.

It was then the *Mademoiselle* herself applied a little powder to Carmella's skin, a faint touch of rouge to her cheeks, and darkened her eye-lashes.

"I cannot wear make-up!" Carmella protested in a shocked voice. "Surely it is only worn by actresses on the stage?"

Mademoiselle laughed.

"*Ma pauvre innocente!* You 'ave obviously not seen Professional Beauties verry close. They all paint and powder, and I am not telling a secret when I say they darken their eye-lashes and their eye-brows! But not so obvious as for ze stage. They want to look beauteeful whatever their age, and Nature is not always kind to women as *Le Bon Dieu* is to ze flowers!"

Carmella laughed as if she could not help it.

"Are you sure you are telling me the truth?"

"I promise you, everyone at ze noble Marquis's party weel secretly, in their bedrooms, put on a leetle lip-salve, a leetle *poudre,* and, of course, play tricks with their eyes and eye-lashes. *Ma Chérie,* you must do the same, unless you weesh to look like yourself!"

"No, no, of course not, I have to help Gerald."

"*Exactement!* But look in ze mirror and we weel call him up to see you."

Mademoiselle Yvonne had been sitting in front of Carmella while she worked on her face and now she moved away so that she could see her reflection.

She was astonished.

She certainly looked very different — so different that for a moment she could hardly believe it was herself.

She looked beautiful — she would have been very stupid if she had not realised that — but much older and yes, the right word was very much more "sophisticated."

"I am sure my brother will be pleased," she said.

"I shall be verry angree eef 'e ees not!" *Mademoiselle* Yvonne replied.

She went to the door and shouted down the stairs:

"Gerald! Gerald!"

35

He must have heard her in the Sitting-Room because Carmella heard him reply:

"What is it?"

"Come upstairs! I want you to meet a verry charmeeng lady, 'oo 'as called to see me."

Carmella heard Gerald coming up the stairs, and rose from the stool to stand waiting for him in the centre of the room.

He came to the door, and there was silence as he looked at Carmella, and the three women waited for his verdict.

"By Jove!" he ejaculated after a moment. "You are a genius, Yvonne, that is what you are! The Marquis will never guess that elegant female is my little sister from the country!"

"That ees what I thought," Yvonne said, "and you are pleased, *mon Cher?*"

"Very pleased," he replied, then added in a low voice: "I will tell you how pleased later."

Yvonne gave him an enigmatic smile, then went back to Carmella's side to say:

"I 'ave been thinking what more I can do for you, and because I am so verry fond of your brother and 'e has been verry kind while my friend away, I am going to send Jeanne with you this weekend, not only to dress you, but to make-up your face, which I am sure you weel never be able to manage by yourself."

"Oh, that is too much!" Carmella cried. "I cannot ask you to do that!"

"I weel do eet!" *Mademoiselle* Yvonne replied. "I shall miss Jeanne, but it weel only be for Saturday and Sunday. You weel be back on Monday, no?"

The last words were a question not to Carmella, but

she was looking at Gerald.

"We shall be back on Monday," he repeated, "and I will come to see you as soon as we return and tell you what happened."

That was obviously what Yvonne wanted to hear, and she smiled at him before she said:

"Now everytheeng ees settled. Jeanne will pack up all ze things you 'ave chosen, and of course, ze bonnets, ze gloves, and ze sunshades to go weeth them, and you must not forget to collect them before you leave."

"I will collect them when I come to say goodbye to you," Gerald said.

It seemed to Carmella there was a meaning in his words which Yvonne understood, for again she gave him a very attractive smile before she said:

"And now, go downstairs while we return your sister to 'erself, very beauteeful, but certainly not in ze taste of *Monsieur* Iceberg, *le Marquis!*"

Gerald laughed before he replied:

"Not much chance of that with Lady Sybil about."

"I admit she ees beauteeful," *Mademoiselle* said, "but not as beauteeful as your sister will be in few years."

Carmella thought how kind she was being, and she only wished her statement was true.

She started to tell *Mademoiselle* that she could never be as fascinating or as clever as she was, when to her surprise as Jeanne started to undo her pink gown, Yvonne followed Gerald out of the bedroom and shut the door behind her.

As she could hear them talking in low voices at the top of the stairs and because she had no wish to eavesdrop, she said to Jeanne:

"It is very kind of you to come with me. I am, in fact, very frightened of staying for the first time in a big house-party with people I have never met before."

"You weel be as beauteeful an' as smart as they are, *M'mselle*," Jeanne replied. *"Mon Papa* used to say when I was a *jeune fille*. It ees a mistake to be afraid of everyone. All men and women are human, an' if you prick them, they bleed!"

Carmella laughed.

"Your father was right! But it is very difficult not to be frightened of strange people."

As she spoke she was thinking not so much of the people, but of the Marquis himself and the Bramforde necklace which, by this time, if Gerald was right, would have been placed for safe-keeping with the Ingleton jewels.

She could only pray that he did not have a secretary or a Manager who was knowledgeable about stones and who would tell him that the necklace was quite valueless.

"Please, God, do not let him find out!" she found herself praying.

"Now, *M'mselle*, you look just like yourself again!" Jeanne interrupted her prayer.

Looking in the mirror, Carmella could see she was back in her pretty but plain gown in which she had arrived, and she looked exactly as she always did.

"I must thank you for being so helpful!" she said to Jeanne.

Then as she thought it was more polite to speak in her own language, she added in French:

"Je vous remercie, c'est bien aimable de votre part."

Jeanne was delighted.

"*M'mselle* speak like a Parisienne. That ees good. We weel talk together while we are in the country and the servants, at least, will not understand what we say."

Carmella gave a little laugh. At the same time she thought: 'More secrets, more deceptions and more lies.' What would her mother think if she knew?

Jeanne opened the door of the bedroom and she found that *Mademoiselle* Yvonne and Gerald must have gone downstairs.

She called his name, and by the time she reached the small hall he was waiting for her.

She saw to her surprise that he did not look quite as neat and tidy as he had when they arrived, and as he said goodbye to *Mademoiselle* Yvonne she noticed that he had a touch of lip-salve on his cheek.

"I shall be waiteeng," Yvonne said softly, "and *mon Cher*, impatiently."

She looked at him in a meaningful manner, and as if Gerald were embarrassed because Carmella was listening, he went quickly through the front door and out to where the Chaise was waiting.

Carmella held out her hand and was also saying "thank-you," and *Mademoiselle* Yvonne kissed her.

"You are a verry sweet lady, *Mademoiselle* Carmella," she said, "and I know your brother is proud of you."

"If I do not let him down, it will be entirely thanks to you!" Carmella replied.

Mademoiselle Yvonne threw out her hands.

"*Non, non!* But when you success, we weel celebrate. You weel come and see me again?"

It was a question.

"Of course!" Carmella replied. "I shall look forward to it."

"So shall I," *Mademoiselle* Yvonne replied, "eef you come."

Carmella did not understand the doubt expressed in the last three words, but she smiled, got into the Chaise, and Gerald waved as they drove off.

Mademoiselle, standing in the doorway, waved back quite regardless of the fact that her diaphanous negligee made her look somewhat inadequately clothed.

"She is very kind," Carmella said as they drove away.

"She is a jolly good sort," Gerald answered, "and I only wish . . ."

He bit back the words he had been about to say while Carmella waited for the end of the sentence.

"What do you wish?" she asked at length.

There was a pause before Gerald replied:

"That I could afford to give her a decent present."

Carmella, however, had the feeling he had been going to say something quite different, but there had seemed no reason for it.

They drove on and Gerald said:

"I have found out that it takes two hours fast driving to reach Ingleton Hall, and we therefore ought to leave soon after two o'clock on Saturday."

"They are expecting us for tea?"

"More likely champagne," Gerald replied. "But you will want time to dress for dinner, and whatever happens, we must not make ourselves conspicuous by being late."

"No, of course not."

"I will arrange with Yvonne," Gerald went on, "that I will take you round to her house after an early luncheon so that you can change from your own clothes into the ones she is providing for you, and arrive looking the part."

"Of course! I had forgotten about that," Carmella said nervously. "But there is also Mama."

"I have thought of that," Gerald replied. "You will say goodbye to Mama at about twelve-thirty, when I collect you, and you will have to make her believe that you are going to stay with some friends of mine for the weekend, who have a daughter of your age and a son of mine."

More lies, Carmella thought in despair, but she knew he was right and her mother must not have the least idea of what was happening.

Then as they drove on she asked after a moment in a small voice:

"Have you thought what I am to be called?"

"Yes, I have," Gerald answered, "and I have decided, because it would be difficult to check, that you will be Irish."

"Irish?" Carmella repeated in surprise. "But why?"

"Because there are a great number of Irish who have titles, but are not as important as English ones. I have taken a lot of trouble to find this out, and you are therefore the widow of an Irish Peer called Lord O'Kerry."

"A...a widow!" Carmella exclaimed. "Why a widow?"

"Do not be stupid," Gerald admonished her. "If you were just 'Miss Somebody or Other,' and look like you will when Yvonne has finished with you, you would either be a 'Cyprian,' whom I could not take to the Marquis's party, or else a boring old maid, whom no one would want to know."

"What is a 'Cyprian'?" Carmella asked.

Gerald realised he had made a mistake.

"It is the name of an actress who has got a rather bad reputation," he said after a pause, "and I think you must have realised by now that the Marquis, unlike some of his contemporaries, only entertains the top people in the Social World, never actresses and that sort of person."

"You mean he would not invite *Mademoiselle* Yvonne to Ingleton Hall?"

"Certainly not!" Gerald exclaimed.

"She seems to know exactly how the Ladies of Fashion and the Beauties you keep talking about look and behave," Carmella observed.

There was a pause, then Gerald said:

"I suppose she is intelligent enough to listen to the conversation of men who know them well, and also she uses her eyes."

He spoke scathingly, as if he thought his sister was being obtuse, and although Carmella thought it strange, she decided it was a mistake to go on asking questions.

"What I want, Gerry, dearest," she said, "is to be quite certain that I do not let you down, and if we do not obtain the necklace, while the very idea of it terrifies me, it will not be my fault!"

"We will get it back somehow," Gerald said.

Carmella knew he had set his chin in the same manner as he did when he was a little boy determined to have his own way.

Then because it all seemed so hopeless and at the

same time she was desperately frightened of what lay ahead, once again she was praying to her father to help them.

chapter three

THE Marquis of Ingleton looked up as his secretary came into the room.

He was writing at a desk that had been made for his grandfather in the reign of George IV and was very elaborate, with gilt feet and exquisitely gilded handles to the drawers.

"I have brought you the table seating for tonight, M'Lord," his secretary said.

He was a middle-aged man who had been an Army Officer and still looked it.

He had been with the Marquis for nearly ten years, and the smooth running of Ingleton Hall and the Marquis's houses in other parts of the country owed everything to his direction.

He held out the seating-plan which was a replica of the Dining-Room table, done in green leather and with a space to insert a card where every guest would be seated.

The Marquis took it from his secretary, and said as he did so:

"Thank you, Maynard, I expect you have worked it out in your usual efficient manner."

"With the exception, M'Lord," Maynard replied, "that I did not know the name of the lady whom Lord Bramforde is bringing with him."

"I did not enquire before I left London," the Marquis

said, "but you can, of course, add it when she arrives."

"I will do that, M'Lord, and I have put Lord Bramforde in the Rose Suite, with the lady the other side of the *Boudoir*."

As if there was no need for him to confirm that this was the correct procedure, the Marquis nodded.

It was an accepted rule at his parties that the people who were discreetly paired should be as near to each other as possible.

Now as he looked at his list of guests he thought to himself there was a sameness about them which was somewhat monotonous.

They had all, with the exception of Lord Bramforde and his friend, been at a house-party the previous weekend, and during the week had met each other at dinner with the Prince of Wales at Marlborough House, with the Devonshires, with the Londonderrys, and the Earl and Countess de Grey.

As his secretary left the room, the Marquis put down the pen with which he had been writing a letter, and stared with unseeing eyes across the delightfully comfortable Study which he had made his own private sanctum.

He had maintained the tradition set by his father and by his grandfather before him that the pictures in the Study should all be by sporting artists who depicted their predilection for sport.

There was a famous study of horses by Stubbs over the mantelpiece, and other pictures by Heron, Aiken, and Sartorius had made one of the Marquis's friends describe it as his "Private Menagerie."

The Marquis had laughed.

"I think I should miss the pictures if they were not

there," he said, "and talking of menageries, I have been wondering if I would establish one here at Ingleton. I believe my great-grandfather kept two cheetahs, and my grandfather brought back a tiger with him from India, which unfortunately, after a hard winter, died."

"I think a menagerie would be a very good idea," his friend had replied, "but it might distract you from your horses, and that would be a mistake!"

The Marquis knew that his stables were considered to be the best in the country, and his race-horses for the last two years had certainly set out to prove that he had no rivals.

Because racing, hunting, and shooting were his main sports, the men whom he considered his closest friends were all sportsmen.

It was more difficult to entertain them in the summer than it was when there was a choice between hunting or shooting to occupy them during the day.

That meant that he was wise, he knew, to make sure they were entertained very effectively by the ladies who were invited especially on their behalf.

In the party that was arriving today there were no husbands and wives together, and the Marquis had taken great trouble to avoid making a *faux pas* in asking one without the other.

He had for instance been forced to work out precisely when Lord Dudley would be attending a race-meeting in another part of the country so that his wife could eagerly accept an invitation without him.

And Lady Beresford, who was exceedingly jealous, had been called to her mother's death-bed, which enabled Lord Charles to come alone.

Everybody on the list had been chosen for a special

reason: so that they could pair off with a man or a woman with whom they were for the moment intimately concerned.

The exception was Lord Bramforde, who had been asked to bring a lady of his own choice with him.

Looking at his name on the seating-plan now, the Marquis frowned.

He thought he had made a mistake in including so young a man in a party where everybody would be much older than he was.

But after he had won such a large sum from him, Lord Bramforde had looked so stunned that for a moment he felt almost guilty about it.

Then he told himself he was being absurdly sentimental, which was something he had no intention of being, and that if Bramforde could not afford to gamble, then he should have the good sense and the will-power not to do so.

'I expect it was the humiliation more than the money,' he thought.

But he wished now he had not given him an invitation, as he did not like strangers at his parties.

He then looked to see who was seated on his right and left at dinner and saw that Lady Sybil was, as he expected, on his right, and Lady Brooke on his left, with Lord Charles Beresford on the other side of her.

He liked Daisy Brooke, as did everybody, and she had been sensational ever since at eighteen she had dazzled London with her beauty and her fortune of over 30,000 pounds a year.

Lord Brooke, the eldest son of the Earl of Warwick, had fallen in love with her at first sight, but when he asked Lord Rosslyn if he might pay his addresses to

47

Daisy, the answer was "no," because Lady Rosslyn had great ambitions for her elder daughter.

She was well aware that Queen Victoria, who was rapidly becoming the "Match-Maker" of Europe, had decided it was a mistake to keep marrying her own children off to penniless German Royalty who demanded large settlements.

She was, in fact, contemplating an English heiress for her youngest son, Prince Leopold, Duke of Albany, and the description of pretty Daisy had aroused the Queen's interest.

Queen Victoria and Lady Rosslyn had actually brought the marriage negotiations to a climax, but when Daisy was taken to stay at Prince Leopold's country house, the eighteen-year-old girl flatly refused his offer.

A few hours later, when walking under an umbrella with Lord Brooke, she happily accepted her second proposal of marriage in one day.

It had all been extremely romantic, and when it leaked out to the gossip press, the news was devoured by the women in every home in the country.

But within five years of her marriage, Daisy, the innocent débutante, the woman the Queen had wanted for her delicate, haemophiliac son, was gazing with admiration at the hero of the moment, a splendid reckless sailor who was a close friend of the Prince of Wales.

In 1884 Lord Charles was in Egypt, organising the transport steamers for the Nile cataracts which were to relieve General Gordon in Khartoum.

Lord Charles, after the Battle of Abu Klea, at which all the Naval Officers except himself were killed, managed to escape and to rescue Sir Charles Wilson's advance detachments, left in isolation after Khartoum fell.

He won the C.B. for this dangerous operation brilliantly carried out under enemy fire.

He had, however, returned to England in July of the following year, when Lady Brooke, as a diligent Victorian wife, was producing a third child for her husband.

There was a celebration with fireworks at her home at Easton Lodge.

Now a year later, when she had produced a son, Daisy was head-over-heels in love with Lord Charles Beresford.

Thinking about them, it suddenly occurred to the Marquis's very astute and intelligent mind that the general loosening of morals which was typified by his party this weekend was wholly due to the Prince of Wales.

It was a blessed relief after enduring twenty-five years of repressive, almost puritanical rules of Society under Queen Victoria, when it was whispered that the handsome Prince of Wales was flirting with and certainly paying court to any beautiful lady who caught his fancy.

His behaviour not only delighted London, but enchanted Europe.

Albert Edward was such an attractive man with so warm a nature that the ladies who surrendered themselves to him did not do so entirely because it had become the smart thing to do.

Even Queen Victoria, who was being difficult with her son, had written:

Bertie is so good with amiable qualities that it makes one forget and overlook much that one would wish different.

* * *

Her Majesty need not have worried. London Society wished nothing different.

They were thrilled at the chance, and for the first time in years it had become possible for gentlemen to contemplate having an *affaire-de-coeur* with a woman of his own class.

All this flashed through the Marquis's mind, and he was aware that the Prince never approached very young women, or wives who had not long been married.

He took pains to conduct his love-affairs with discretion and expected his friends to do the same thing.

Looking again at his list of guests, the Marquis knew there would be no scandals, no unpleasant gossip, and he could almost guarantee no hard feelings.

At the same time, he was asking himself, although it seemed a strange thing to do, what was the end of it all?

Already two of his friends in the party had been the lovers of several of the great Beauties who filled the magazines and newspapers, and had now embarked on yet another romance which would end in exactly the same way as their others.

Thinking about it, the Marquis knew, if he was honest, that he was, although he was trying not to admit it, becoming bored with Lady Sybil Greeson.

The daughter of the Duke of Dorset, she had made an unfortunate marriage with a man whose only real interest in life was fishing.

Once she had given him two sons, Lord Greeson abandoned all pretence of spending his time with his wife, who had blossomed into a sensational Beauty.

He went from river to river at the right seasons of the year intent only on beating his own and everybody else's record for the number of salmon and trout he caught.

It was inevitable therefore that Lady Sybil should, of course with discretion, take one lover after another, until, when she met the Marquis of Ingleton, she was aware she had met her fate.

She fell in love for the first time in her life, wildly, tempestuously, and with a fierce possessiveness which defeated its own end.

To the Marquis, like shooting, fishing, and racing, women were a pleasure which should not encroach on his other interests.

They had to take their place in his life, to be dispensed with when he no longer found them as alluring as they had seemed at first.

He was so awe-inspiring, that it made women keep themselves under control, even while finding him an irresistible challenge, because he was so elusive.

It was however impossible for Lady Sybil to realise how foolish she was being.

"I love you, Tyrone!" she had cried passionately when last he was with her. "Why can I not be with you, not only occasionally, but always and for ever?"

The Marquis had heard this question before and he did not bother to reply.

At the time he was dressing himself neatly and methodically in front of the mirror over the mantelpiece in Lady Sybil's bedroom.

She was lying back against the silk pillows, her perfect body glowing like a translucent pearl, her red hair falling over her white shoulders.

Lady Sybil could have posed for a picture of any of

the numerous Venuses beloved of the Romans.

Yet the Marquis's eyes as he saw her reflection in the mirror were hard.

Although she was not aware of it, he was thinking that it was always a mistake for a woman to be unrestrained and demandingly passionate at the moment when the fires of love had died down.

He finished arranging his tie, shrugged himself into his evening-coat which was lying on an armchair, and turned towards the bed to say:

"Go to sleep, Sybil, and stop worrying your pretty head with idiotic questions that are quite unanswerable."

"Are you quite certain they are?" Lady Sybil asked with a sob in her voice.

"It is too late for conundrums," the Marquis replied, and picking up her arm which she had flung in an abandoned way across the bed, he kissed it perfunctorily and moved towards the door.

"Stay, Tyrone! Stay a little longer!" Lady Sybil begged.

"I will see you on Friday," he said, "and I will send a carriage for you after luncheon."

"But I must see you before that...!" Lady Sybil cried.

Before she had completed half the sentence, however, the door of her bedroom shut and she heard the Marquis going down the stairs, where a sleepy night-footman would be waiting in the hall to let him out of the front-door.

It was then she gave a little cry of exasperation and turned over to hide her face in her pillow.

It was always the same, she thought: when the Marquis left her, she felt frustrated because he would not stay longer.

At the same time, although she dared not admit it, she was apprehensive in case she never saw him again.

She had tried so hard, so desperately hard to capture him completely.

But she knew, if she was honest, that while she could excite him and while he was the most ardent and irresistible lover she had ever known, she had not touched his heart, and that nothing she could say or do could hold him as she wanted him held.

Any other woman on whom the Marquis had bestowed his favours could have told her that they felt the same, that there was an elusive quality about Tyrone Ingleton which they had never found in any other man.

It was almost as if he delighted in being out of reach, and had an omnipotent way of treating everybody, even the women who loved him, so that, God-like, he towered above them, while although they hated to admit it they grovelled at his feet.

"I love him! I love him!" Lady Sybil murmured over and over again.

And yet she knew that nothing she could say or do would prevent him from behaving exactly as he wished, and it was useless to expect him to be any different.

Many people, not only women, had wondered why the Marquis had such a contemptuous attitude towards the world in which he lived and the people with whom he associated.

"The trouble with you, Ingleton," one of his friends had said to him, "is that you have too much. You are too rich, too important, too successful, and far too intelligent ever to be content with ordinary mortals like us!"

"I cannot think why you should say that," the Marquis replied aggressively.

"It is true," his friend protested. "I think the only time I have ever known you to be human is when we were in India together, and in such dangerous situations that I often wonder now how it was possible that we survived."

The Marquis laughed.

"It was then I was human?"

"To me you were," his friend replied, "and I have never forgotten how much I relied on you, or how grateful I am because you saved my life."

Because the conversation was causing him embarrassment, the Marquis had changed the subject, yet now in an introspective mood he found himself wondering why he had been more human then than he was now.

He could not find a ready answer, and he therefore returned to his letter-writing.

But he also had the uncomfortable feeling that he was not going to enjoy his house-party this weekend as much as he had hoped.

Driving out of London, Gerald, who was extremely proficient with the reins, glanced at Carmella sitting beside him and thought that Yvonne had been brilliant in the way she had altered her whole appearance.

He knew his sister looked exceedingly smart in exactly the right clothes for a Lady of Fashion to arrive in at a smart house-party.

The Viscount Turnleigh might be a pompous bore, which he undoubtedly was, but he was generous when it suited his own interests.

He paid Yvonne's bills without protest, not only at

the very best Bond Street dressmakers, but for the gowns she ordered from Paris and which were undeniably smarter and more elegant than anything that could be procured in London.

Carmella looked exactly as he wanted her to look, but he was aware, because he knew her so well, that she was very apprehensive and frightened.

It was not only that she might fail him in this masquerade, but that also they would not be able to steal the necklace.

Gerald found himself thinking that everything would have been very much easier if he could have taken Yvonne with him.

He knew that at a large number of noblemen's parties that would have been easy.

One member of White's he knew gave enormous parties at his country estate for the Gaiety Girls and their Protectors, besides any outstanding ballerina or actress who was being kept by his particular friends.

But the Marquis was different; so different that Gerald was aware that if he had done anything so indiscreet as not to bring a Lady to Ingleton Hall, he would have been asked to leave, and there would have been no question of his staying as the Marquis's guest until Monday.

"There was no one else I could turn to," he told himself.

Then because he had a happy-go-lucky nature which made him believe always that his luck would turn, that the sun would shine and things were never as disastrous as they seemed, he told himself that he and Mella would pull it off.

He looked at her and smiled, then he said:

"I suppose you realise we would have looked very silly if Yvonne had not realised at the last moment that you would need some jewellery?"

"I had never thought of it," Carmella replied, "but of course a married woman, or rather, a widow, even of an Irish Peer would own something in the way of jewellery."

"Well, for goodness' sake, do not lose Yvonne's diamonds. It would cost us a fortune."

Carmella looked at him wide-eyed.

"Who could have given her anything so valuable?"

She paused, then she asked in a tone of horror:

"It was not you, Gerry?"

"No, of course not!" Gerald replied. "Where would I get the money to buy a necklace like that? I could not even afford one stone of it!"

"Now you are making me frightened! Suppose I lose it?"

"Jeanne will look after it," Gerald said blithely. "All you have to do is to put it round your neck and make all the other women envious, although of course they will have as good, if not better, in their family collections."

Carmella had not replied for a moment, then she said:

"Who could have given *Mademoiselle* Yvonne such magnificent diamonds?"

"Tony, of course," Gerald replied. "He is as rich as Croesus!"

There was no mistaking the envy in his voice and he drove on in silence for some while.

Then Carmella said:

"You love *Mademoiselle* Yvonne, do you not, Gerald?"

Her brother did not reply but she saw his lips tighten and she said quickly:

"I . . . I should not have . . . asked."

"That is true enough," Gerald admitted, "but if you want to know, Carmella, I find her very alluring as well as very understanding and sympathetic, and I think she loves me a little."

"I think so too," Carmella said, "but you could not afford to marry her."

"Marry her? There is no question of that!"

Carmella looked surprised.

"If you could afford it, would you marry *Mademoiselle?*"

"Of course not," Gerald replied, "and you must not ask awkward questions. Because you have been living in the country, you do not understand that it is not a question of marriage where somebody like Yvonne is concerned."

Carmella was about to say she still did not understand, but Gerald went on:

"You must be aware that Mama would be very shocked at your meeting somebody like Yvonne, and horrified if she knew you were wearing her clothes and borrowing her jewels. It is something which no one, and I mean *no one*, Mella, must ever know! Now do you understand?"

"Yes, Gerry, and I will not talk about it again."

Carmella did not really understand, but she knew her brother was upset and she did not want to make him any more apprehensive than he was already before they reached Ingleton Hall.

They drove for quite a long way in silence, then Gerry said:

57

"I was thinking it over last night, that you have never been to Ireland and if people ask you questions you might make a mess of it."

He went on as if he was thinking it over.

"So I think you must say that while your husband was Irish, you met him here in England, and as you had very little money, you settled down in Gloucestershire, where he had a hunting accident."

"Which killed him," Carmella murmured as if she were memorising the story.

"Yes!" Gerry agreed. "And you remained on for two years after his death, and now at last you have come to London."

Because of the way he spoke and the manner in which he had it planned out, Carmella was certain that *Mademoiselle* Yvonne had had a hand in inventing the story.

But she thought it would be a mistake to say so, and she merely remarked:

"I will remember what you suggest and it will certainly make it much easier. At least I know I can talk about Gloucestershire without making any mistakes."

Gerry laughed.

"That is true enough."

They drove on, and only when they turned in at the magnificent wrought-iron gates that had heraldic stone lions at the sides of them, did Carmella feel that her hands were cold, her lips were dry, and there were butterflies fluttering inside her breast.

"I say, it is jolly impressive!" Gerry exclaimed as they drove down a long drive of ancient oak trees, and saw at the end an enormous Georgian house with a wing on either side of a centre block.

There were Ionic pillars supporting a portico at the top of a long flight of stone steps, and statues and urns decorating the roof of the building were silhouetted against the sky along with the Marquis's special standard which was flying in a slight breeze.

At the front of the house was an enormous lake on which, as they drew nearer, Carmella could see swans, both black and white, sailing serenely over the silver water.

"It is lovely! Perfectly lovely!" she exclaimed. "And oh, Gerry, it is exactly what you should have!"

"It is exactly what I have got!" Gerald said truculently. "If only I had the money with which to improve it!"

Because Carmella knew it hurt him to talk of the home he had been forced to abandon, she said quickly:

"You must look after me, Gerry, and see that I do not make any mistakes. You know how ignorant I am of the sort of people we will meet, and I am sure from what you said that the Marquis will be very frightening!"

"He is!" Gerry agreed. "And you must not forget for a moment while you are here to be very careful of how you speak to me in public."

"I had not thought of that," Carmella said. "How should I address you?"

"I believe most people are very formal," Gerald said, "but as I am going to say you are a distant cousin of mine, you should call me 'Gerald,' and I will call you 'Carmella.'"

"If you had called me anything else, I should never have remembered it," Carmella said. "As it is, I keep saying to myself: 'I am Lady O'Kerry! I am Lady O'Kerry! And my husband is dead!'"

She glanced down at her hand as she spoke and knew that underneath the very elegant suede glove which Yvonne had lent her was her mother's wedding-ring.

Her mother had been suffering recently with a touch of arthritis, and because her fingers were slightly swollen she had removed her wedding-ring and asked Carmella to put it in a safe place.

Last night Carmella had slipped it onto her own finger and found that it fitted exactly.

She therefore put it carefully in her purse until she reached *Mademoiselle* Yvonne's house after luncheon, and had then put it on.

When she arrived to change her clothes, *Mademoiselle* Yvonne had said:

"I see, *Mademoiselle*, you have a wedding-ring. I worried in case you did not think of it, for it's sometheeng which I cannot supply."

She spoke a little wistfully, and Carmella wondered if she would like to be married, but was too shy to ask her.

While she was changing, Gerald was having luncheon downstairs with *Mademoiselle* Yvonne, and when they offered Carmella something to eat, she said she had already had luncheon at home.

She however accepted a small glass of champagne because, as *Mademoiselle* Yvonne said, it would stop her from feeling tired on the journey and frightened when she arrived.

Now as she stepped out of the Chaise and saw footmen running a red carpet down the steps, she felt very frightened indeed and wanted to hold on to Gerry.

He, however, having handed over the reins to the

groom, walked up the steps proudly, with his head in the air, looking, Carmella had to admit, very smart and every inch a Lord.

'At least he does not have to pretend,' she thought with relief.

As they entered the hall, a footman came forward to remove the light travelling-coat she had worn over her gown to prevent it from being covered with dust.

Actually there had not been very much dust, since it had rained the previous evening, and she knew that Gerry had arranged that if it was in fact a wet day, they would travel to Ingleton Hall in a closed carriage rather than by Chaise.

"Who lends you all these carriages and horses?" she asked.

There was a pause before Gerry replied:

"Tony told me before he went to the country that I could exercise his horses if I wished to, and Yvonne arranged that I should use his Chaise or his carriage if she did not need it herself."

It seemed to Carmella that the Viscount was a very accommodating man, and very generous with his possessions.

She could not help wondering if, as he was obviously fond of *Mademoiselle* Yvonne, he was not jealous of Gerry spending so much time with her, and making himself very much at home when it came to drinking his champagne and using his carriages and his servants.

But she knew it was a mistake to ask too many questions which might annoy Gerry, so she said nothing.

At the same time she could not help wondering about it.

* * *

The Hall was most impressive, with a beautiful carved and gilt staircase rising on one side of it.

There seemed to Carmella to be a remarkable number of servants wearing what she supposed was the Ingleton livery, and a very impressive Butler with white hair led them to the double doors of what she supposed was the Drawing-Room.

She was to find later it was only a small Salon, while the large Drawing-Room was on the next floor, but it looked very impressive to Carmella.

As she entered, the crystal chandeliers and the hothouse flowers in tall vases that scented the air made everything swim before her eyes.

She found it hard to focus on a group of people at the far end of the room in front of a fireplace.

The Butler had asked her name and he announced now:

"Lord Bramforde and Lady O'Kerry, M'Lord!"

One man detached himself from the group and came towards them, and as he did so, Carmella knew from Gerry's description of him that this was the Marquis.

Never had she seen a man who was so handsome, and also walked in a way which made him appear taller than he was and overwhelmingly authoritative.

He reached them and Gerry held out his hand as the Marquis said:

"I am delighted to see you, Bramforde. You did not have difficulty in finding your way here from London?"

"No, indeed," Gerry replied, "it was very easy, thanks to the instructions your secretary sent me."

"Good!" the Marquis said.

"I have brought with me..." Gerry began, and Carmella realised he was a little nervous, "a distant cousin of mine, Lady O'Kerry."

The Marquis held out his hand.

"I am delighted you could join us, Lady O'Kerry."

"It is very kind of you to have me," Carmella answered conventionally.

As she spoke she realised that the Marquis was looking at her with hard, penetrating eyes that seemed, she thought, to look beneath the surface, and to see quite clearly that she was not what she pretended to be.

Then she told herself she was being needlessly apprehensive and as Gerry said, she had to "think" herself into the part.

If she appeared nervous or frightened, it might arouse the marquis's suspicions.

"I cannot imagine why we have not met before, Lady O'Kerry," the Marquis was saying. "I feel you cannot have been in London for long."

"No, indeed," Carmella replied. "I have been in mourning for the past year and living very quietly in Gloucestershire."

"Ah, now I understand," he said. "But I am sure London will welcome you and you will find it impossible to live very quietly in the future."

Carmella smiled to show she appreciated what he was saying, and the Marquis led them across the room to introduce them to his friends.

Only four other people had arrived before them, and because Carmella was feeling agitated, she did not hear their names clearly.

She only knew that both the ladies were very beautiful and very smartly dressed in the same way that she was.

In fact, *Mademoiselle* Yvonne had been right, for she was not in the least overdressed.

The men were both distinguished and titled, but older, and one of them said to the Marquis:

"You did not tell us, Ingleton, that you were producing a new beauty to bemuse and bewilder us poor mortals!"

Because the way he spoke seemed more amusing than embarrassing, Carmella did not blush, she merely remarked:

"That is a very kind thing to say, but Gerald has been telling me all the way here how beautiful His Lordship's lady guests would be, and how distinguished the gentlemen."

"Now you are flattering me, Lady O'Kerry!" the Gentleman said.

The Marquis was about to say something, when the Butler announced:

"Lady Brooke and Lord Charles Beresford!"

Because Carmella had read so much about the beautiful Lady Brooke in *The Ladies Journal* and seen her picture, she was thrilled to have the chance to meet her.

She had, in fact, not expected her to be so small or so lovely.

The moment she arrived, the tempo seemed to rise, and it was impossible for anyone to look at anybody else when Daisy was laughing, teasing the Marquis, and at the same time giving Lord Charles intimate looks from under her eye-lashes, which seemed to Carmella to be very indiscreet.

Because she was very perceptive, she realised that Lady Brooke was reckless as well as beautiful, and when she fell in love, she threw caution to the winds.

She certainly made it clear that Lord Charles, who was much older than she was, was her possession, and yet she was so lovely, so charming to everybody, that it was impossible to criticise her behaviour.

As more people arrived, Carmella was aware the men were all much older than Gerald, and the women than she was.

They had so much to say to each other, being all old friends, that she felt she had escaped their notice.

She was relieved, after they had had a very elaborate tea brought in by several footmen, that the ladies were expected to go upstairs and rest before dinner.

The Marquis, appearing to be the perfect host, escorted Carmella with two other ladies to the foot of the stairs.

"You are in your usual room," he said to one of them, "and you, Daisy, are in the Queen's Suite."

"Which is the one I like best, Tyrone," Daisy Brooke replied. "You are an angel, and let me tell you, I adore being back at Ingleton."

"How could I say anything but that I adore having you here?" the Marquis replied.

Then he said to Carmella:

"My Housekeeper will show you to the Rose Suite, where you will be, and I hope very comfortable, Lady O'Kerry."

"Thank you," Carmella answered.

She had the feeling that he was looking at her in the same penetrating manner that he had when she arrived.

She however hurried up the stairs, holding herself in what she hoped was a dignified manner, as if she were quite used to being in such a large house and with such impressive company.

Only when she found Jeanne waiting for her in the Rose Bedroom and the door was shut did she say in French:

"What do you think of it, Jeanne?"

"Verry impressive, *M'mselle,* and exactly what you'd expect of a Milord. If only *M'mselle* could be here to see it!"

"I wished that too, when I started," Carmella said honestly.

Then as she knew that, for the moment it was very exciting to be in such a marvellous house, to meet people who until now had been only names in newspapers and magazines, and to be surrounded with a luxury she had never dreamt of when they lived in Gloucestershire.

Yet when she thought of the Marquis she gave a little shiver.

She was certain she and Gerry would have to be very clever if they were to continue to deceive him.

As to being able to steal the necklace—she could not bear to think of it.

"If the Marquis ever found out what we were doing, it would be utterly and completely disastrous!" she told herself.

As Jeanne began to unbutton her gown at the back, she knew that she was shivering, and once again her lips were dry because she was so frightened.

chapter four

AFTER she had bathed in scented water Carmella said to Jeanne:

"What do I wear tonight?"

"Not the best gown," Jeanne replied, "because it is Friday."

Carmella looked at her for an explanation and Jeanne said:

"First night everybody is fatigued, go to bed early. Saturday night all ees verry gay, verry late an' everybody wear their verry best."

Carmella laughed because it sounded so funny. Then she asked:

"How do you know all this, Jeanne?"

As she spoke she thought it strange that *Mademoiselle* Yvonne's maid should be so knowledgeable about what was correct in a house as grand as that owned by the Marquis.

Jeanne smiled.

"When I first come to England, *Mademoiselle*, I'm lady's-maid to Dowager Countess, verry grand, verry important."

Carmella was intrigued.

"Why did you not stay with her?"

"Verry dull, we spend all time in ze country, and houses verry cold. I shiver an' shiver an' wish I back in *Paree*."

Carmella laughed again.

"And you find it much more amusing with *Mademoiselle*?"

"*Oui, oui!*" Jeanne agreed. "I like London. Now I have many, many friends."

Carmella thought it was a blessing that Jeanne knew "the ropes" as Gerry would say, while she did not.

Then she remembered and said:

"You must be careful, Jeanne, to speak to me as 'My Lady.'"

"Quite right, *Mademoiselle*, I careful," Jeanne agreed, "and so I not forget, I call you M'Lady when we are alone."

"I think that is a good idea," Carmella said, "and that will prevent me from forgetting too."

Jeanne did her hair in the same elegant fashion she had arranged it before she left London, then helped her into a very pretty gown which had come from Paris.

It was a blue that suited *Mademoiselle* Yvonne's red hair and was therefore not a bright colour, but soft and seductive like the sky over the sea.

It made Carmella look very ethereal, and at the same time, she thought, when she looked in the mirror, very young.

"Perhaps I would look better wearing the necklace," she suggested.

To her surprise, Jeanne shook her head.

"*Non*, not tonight, M'Lady, the necklace is too grand for Friday night, an' you have only one set, other ladies will have different set each night."

"Then what shall I wear?" Carmella asked.

"Footman bring flowers," Jeanne replied.

Sure enough, as she was just putting the finishing touches to Carmella's hair, there was a knock on the door, and when Jeanne opened it, she spoke to somebody outside.

She came back to Carmella with a tray on which there was arranged corsages of all the most beautiful flowers imaginable.

There were orchids, camelias, gardenias, and roses, besides lilies-of-the-valley and little clusters of hothouse flowers to which Carmella could not put a name.

She looked at them in surprise, but Jeanne knew exactly what was required.

Taking two corsages of white orchids spotted with pink, she handed the tray back to the servant outside the door.

First she pinned a corsage of the orchids onto Carmella's hair, making it look like a tiara.

Then, taking one orchid from the other corsage, she produced a narrow strip of velvet in the same colour as the gown, and having pinned the orchid to it, she tied it round Carmella's neck.

The result was certainly original, and, Carmella thought, very French. It made it quite unnecessary for her, for tonight at any rate, to wear jewels.

"You are clever, Jeanne!" she exclaimed.

"I think idea on the way down," Jeanne replied, "and I know M'Lady be different from all ze other ladies downstairs."

Carmella wondered if this might be a mistake, then there was another knock, but this time not on the door to the passage, but on a door she had hardly noticed which was beside a window at the far end of the room.

When Jeanne went to open it, it was Gerry, who stood there looking very resplendent in his new evening-clothes.

"Are you ready?" he asked. "I thought you would like me to take you down."

"But of course!" Carmella replied. "I would be very nervous if I had to go alone."

As he came into the room she said:

"Are you sleeping in the next room?"

"We have a *boudoir* between our rooms which is correct."

"Correct for what?"

There was a little pause, then Gerry replied:

"In house-parties they usually put people who are friends near to each other."

"That is kind," Carmella smiled, "especially for somebody shy like me."

She did not notice that Gerry glanced at Jeanne as if to warn her, while Jeanne made a little gesture which told him she understood.

"Let me look at you," Gerry said.

Carmella turned round to face him, watching his expression anxiously in case he disapproved.

"You look fantastic!" he exclaimed. "And no one would suspect for a moment that Lady O'Kerry is my little sister."

"I hope not," Carmella replied. "It will be humiliating if we have gone to all this trouble for nothing."

As she spoke she could not help thinking that they had to be careful of the Marquis.

She could still feel his eyes probing into her as if he looked for something, although she had no idea what it could be.

"Now, come along," Gerry said, "we must not be late for dinner."

"When you come up to bed, M'Lady," Jeanne said, "pull bell on right side of fireplace. Eet rings in my bedroom, and so I come to you quick."

'The Marquis thinks of everything that concerns his guests,' Carmella thought.

As she walked down the stairs beside Gerry, she knew that, however sophisticated she might appear outwardly, inside she felt shy and nervous of making a mistake.

The room in which they assembled before dinner was larger and much more impressive than that in which the Marquis had received them.

The house-party had certainly grown since Carmella went upstairs to rest.

Now there were several more beautiful women, and as they were not yet all downstairs, there were more gentlemen than ladies.

While she was introduced to them all once again, Carmella still found it difficult to remember their names.

One man in particular seemed to her outstanding, whose name was Harry Cust, which was not difficult for her to remember.

She learned that he was attached to the Countess de Grey, who Carmella knew without being told was one of the famous Beauties.

She was tall and dark, and Carmella thought she looked like one of the large black swans she had seen on the lake as they arrived.

It was obvious that she made a perfect pair with Harry Cust, who was fair, very handsome, and had the most striking blue eyes Carmella had ever seen.

Because the Countess de Grey behaved very possessively with Mr. Cust, Carmella thought they must be engaged to be married, and she asked the gentleman on one side of her at dinner if the Countess was a widow.

"A widow!" he exclaimed. "Not at the moment, although she has been one. Now she is married to the best game-shot in England."

He chuckled as he said:

"You must ask our host about him. He is reputed never to just wing a bird, and is so accurate he always hits them in the head."

"Then he is indeed a very good shot," Carmella said. "I hate to think of birds being wounded and left to die slowly because they cannot be picked up."

She knew it was something her father disliked too, and he would spend a long time with the dogs looking for a bird that could not be accounted for when a pheasant drive was over.

The gentleman next to Carmella seemed for a moment to be deep in his thoughts, then he said with a chuckle:

"I will tell you a rather amusing story about the Countess's first husband."

Carmella listened intently as he went on:

"He was the fourth Earl of Lonsdale, and being very keen on yachting, he often left Gladys, who is very beautiful, as you can see, alone to amuse herself."

Looking across the table at the Countess de Grey, Carmella thought she was indeed very beautiful.

At the same time, she had the feeling, although of course she did not say so, that she was a rather hard, ruthless woman with whom she would find it impossible to be friends.

"Strangely enough," the gentleman was continuing, "it was Gladys who was in the South of France when Lonsdale died unexpectedly, not in his own house, but in one which he rented so that he could entertain the actresses to whom he often gave supper-parties."

Carmella's eyes widened, as she thought it seemed a strange thing to do, then she supposed the Earl of Lonsdale rented a house to which people like *Mademoiselle* Yvonne would be invited.

Her informant gave another chuckle as he said:

"Because it took Gladys a day and a night to return home from Monte Carlo, the Earl's body for the sake of respectability was smuggled in a cab from where he had died back to the Lonsdale mansion in Carlton House Terrace!"

He laughed uproariously at what seemed to him a tremendous joke, and with an effort Carmella managed a smile.

It seemed to her quite extraordinary that a man who was married to anyone as beautiful as the Countess de Grey would want to give supper-parties for actresses, and to rent a house in which to do it seemed even more extraordinary.

Then she found herself wondering, as *Mademoiselle* Yvonne was living in that elegant house in St. John's Wood which must belong to the Viscount Turnleigh, whether the Viscount also had a wife.

If that was so, it seemed very shocking.

She looked round the table, and seeing how intent everybody was in talking to the beautiful lady next to

73

them, she found herself questioning how many of the gentlemen who looked so smart and so very distinguished had wives elsewhere.

Alternatively how many of the ladies had husbands who were perhaps yachting, racing, or intent on other pleasures rather than being with their wives.

To Carmella everything seemed incomprehensible, and she began to understand why it was impossible for Gerry to bring an unmarried woman to the party knowing that a young girl, like herself, would be very shocked.

"I am shocked," she thought.

Yet she knew it was quite immaterial what she felt beside the fact that she had to help Gerry get back the Bramforde necklace.

The gentleman who had told her the amusing story about the Earl of Lonsdale was now deeply engrossed with the very attractive lady on his other side.

Because she knew it was rude to sit silent, Carmella turned to Gerry.

"Do you know who everybody is?" she asked.

Gerry grinned.

"I know them by reputation, but I am not privileged as a rule to be in this sort of party."

"Are they all very grand and very rich?"

"They are both those things and a great deal more," he said. "You see before you the cream of London Society, the 'Marlborough House Set' which you have heard talked about in whispers! As being here is something we are never likely to do again, you should make the most of it!"

"I am trying to," Carmella replied, "but you know it is frightening for me."

Gerry frowned as if he were afraid somebody would overhear what she had said, then lowering his voice he remarked:

"Be very careful and do not forget to find out what we want to know."

Carmella's heart gave a little jump.

Coming down in the Chaise he had said to her:

"What we have to find out one way or another is where the Marquis keeps his safe. I dare say Jeanne could do that better than we can. At the same time, we have no wish to confide in her."

"No, of course not!" Carmella agreed. "But perhaps I could talk about the Ingleton jewels."

"That is a good idea," Gerry answered, "but for God's sake be tactful, and do not make anybody suspicious after the necklace has disappeared that you have it."

Carmella thought they would be very, very lucky to be able to spirit the necklace away without anybody being aware of it.

She was certain that when Monday came she and Gerry would drive back to London dismally aware that they had failed utterly in what they had set out to do.

But there was no point in saying so and upsetting her brother more than he was already.

Looking round the table at the exquisite jewels every woman except herself was wearing, Carmella was sure every possible precaution had been taken to ensure that they were not stolen either in their own houses, or in the Marquis's.

After a delicious dinner, the ladies left the Dining-Room and returned to the Drawing-Room, where they had sat before.

Now Carmella saw with a sinking of her heart that at one end of the room a number of card-tables had been set up, and she was afraid that Gerry would once again be foolish enough to gamble.

She thought, although she was not sure, that he was drinking quite a lot at dinner.

There were different wines for every course, and although she had sipped only a little champagne, she was afraid that Gerry might once again become reckless enough to gamble with money he did not possess.

Because she must have been looking worried and a little lost, Lady Brooke, who Carmella was to learn was always kind to strangers, while the other ladies in the same Set were either indifferent or hostile, said to her:

"Come and tell me about yourself, Lady O'Kerry. I do not think we have ever been in the same party before."

"No, I have only just come to London," Carmella replied. "I have been living since my husband ... died, very quietly in the ... country."

"Then I am not being clairvoyant when I predict you will have a very gay and amusing time," Lady Brooke said. "You are beautiful, and I admire the original way in which you have used our host's orchids."

"They are so pretty," Carmella said, "and I do not own much jewellery."

"I expect that is something that time will remedy." Lady Brooke smiled.

They were still talking together when the gentlemen joined them, and the Marquis came across to where they were sitting.

"I meant to tell you at dinner, Daisy," he said, "I have some new horses I want you to see, and one in particular which I think will prove an outstanding hunter."

"Then I certainly want to see it," Lady Brooke exclaimed. "I suppose you have arranged for us to ride tomorrow."

"Any time you want," the Marquis said.

He then looked at Carmella and added:

"As you have been living in the country, Lady O'Kerry, I am sure you enjoy riding?"

"I love it," Carmella said, "but I never thought... I never imagined I should have the... opportunity of riding here and I have not brought a habit with me!"

She sounded so disappointed that Daisy Brooke, who always wanted to help those less fortunate than herself, said at once:

"We are about the same size, Lady O'Kerry, and I will lend you one of mine. I will tell my maid tonight to bring it along to your room."

"That is very kind of you," Carmella replied, "but I do not want to be any trouble."

"It is no trouble, I assure you!" Daisy Brooke replied. "But Tyrone, I do not intend to ride very early. We are all tired after so many Balls this week, and Charlie needs a rest."

"You can ride my horses whenever you like," the Marquis said, "and the same applies to you, Lady O'Kerry. Just tell your maid to inform one of the footmen that you want a horse, or, if you prefer, pick one out from the stables yourself, and I feel you will not be disappointed."

"I am sure I will not," Carmella smiled, "and thank you very, very much. It was stupid of me, but I never thought of anything so wonderful as that I would be allowed to ride your horses."

She spoke in an excited, eager way, which made her sound very young, and the Marquis gave her a penetrating glance before he said:

"Now I must see who wishes to play cards."

Carmella realised that Lady Brooke had already gone to the side of Lord Charles Beresford, and was aware that she and the Marquis were standing a little apart from the others.

She hesitated, then because she could not help herself, she said in a low voice:

"Please, may I ask you . . . something?"

"Of course," he replied, "what is wrong?"

"There is nothing . . . wrong," Carmella replied, "but . . . do not let Gerald gamble."

The Marquis looked surprised. Then he said:

"You are thinking of his bad luck the other night. Well, I really asked him here so that he could have his revenge."

"No, no!" Carmella said frantically. "Please . . . do not encourage him. He has . . . promised not to gamble again . . . and he cannot afford it."

She thought as she spoke it was an indiscreet thing to say and Gerry would be angry with her.

But she knew he would not be strong enough to refuse to play cards if the Marquis invited him to.

She had no idea as she looked up at her host that her eyes were pleading frantically with him to understand, and her whole body was tense.

He looked at her for a long moment before he said:

"Because I want you to enjoy your first visit to my house, Lady O'Kerry, I will do as you say, and I will somehow contrive that Bramforde does not play cards this evening."

"Thank you... thank you," Carmella replied, "and you will not let him know I asked you?"

"No, of course not," the Marquis said.

There was a twist to his lips as he spoke, as if he were amused by the anxiety in her voice.

Then as he walked away Carmella knew that if Gerry found out what she had said, he would be very angry with her.

"He would think it humiliating," she told herself, "at the same time, he cannot lose any more money."

As if he knew it was expected of him, Gerry, who had been deep in conversation with another man, came across the room towards her.

"Everybody is going to play cards," he said in a low voice.

"Oh, Gerry, you promised you would not do so!"

"But what can I do? What can I say?" he asked. "I shall look like a fool if I am the only man sitting out."

Then, as Carmella looked frantically across the room, wondering if the Marquis would really help her, he came towards them with another man walking beside him.

"Do you feel like giving Sir Robert a game of billiards, Bramforde?" he asked. "He tells me he is bored with cards."

"I would enjoy a game very much," Gerry answered quickly.

Sir Robert, whom Carmella remembered hearing Gerry talk about, held out his hand and said to Carmella:

"I am delighted to meet you, Lady O'Kerry. We were introduced before dinner, but I did not realise you were with Bramforde."

"He has told me how very kind you have been to him at the Club," Carmella said.

"I am an old member, and he has just joined," Sir Robert answered, "and I can remember when I was Bramforde's age feeling very nervous, until I found my feet."

As he spoke, a very pretty woman wearing a great many diamonds slipped her arm through his.

"I hear you are going to play billiards," she said. "I will allow you one game, Robert, then I want to take you to the Conservatory."

Sir Robert looked down at her with an expression on his face which Carmella thought was one of infatuation.

It seemed strange to her in anyone so old, for she was quite certain that Sir Robert was the same age as her father.

Then he said good-humouredly:

"Very well, Dolly, one game, then naturally, I will do as you tell me."

"I shall come to watch," Dolly said, "and make certain you do not cheat!"

Sir Robert and Gerry laughed, as if this were an impossibility.

Then because she was afraid they might go without her, Carmella said:

"Please, may I come too?"

"You can hardly expect us to leave you behind," Sir Robert said. "Besides, you will want to keep an eye on Bramforde, and see that *he* does not cheat!"

They walked towards the Drawing-Room door, and

as they passed the Marquis, Carmella gave him a smile to show how grateful she was that he had arranged things so cleverly, and she thought for a moment there was a faint twinkle in his hard eyes.

His lips however still looked cynical and she wondered what he was thinking and if, in fact, she had done Gerry harm in any way by asking his assistance.

The Billiard-Room was only a short distance from the Drawing-Room, and was magnificent, as was everything else in the house.

The table was beautifully lighted, and all round the room there were comfortable sofas and chairs from which people could watch those who were playing.

As Sir Robert and Gerry picked up their cues, Dolly, whose full name Carmella had still not heard, said:

"I cannot think why Robert always wants to do something different from everybody else! It would be more fun for us upstairs, and if they are playing Roulette, I want to play too."

She spoke petulantly, then she said:

"I expect there will be a big party tomorrow night, then we shall have our chance."

"I have never played Roulette," Carmella said.

"Oh, it is not a difficult thing to learn," Dolly laughed, "and it is always rather fun at these sorts of parties, when it is an understood rule that if the ladies are lucky, they keep their winnings, but if they lose, their partner, whoever that may be, pays."

Carmella thought in horror that Gerry must not play Roulette either, and she found herself wishing fervently they had not come to the party.

She was quite certain that by Sunday night the whole thing would be a fiasco, with Gerry owing more money than he did already, and then travelling back to London without the necklace.

Sir Robert and Gerry's game seemed to take a long time, until Dolly, who had been talking about herself and the difficulty of buying really beautiful clothes in London, sprang up with delight and carried Sir Robert off to see the Conservatory.

As soon as they had left the Billiard-Room, Carmella said to Gerry in a conspiratorial whisper:

"That lady said they would be playing Roulette tomorrow night."

"I know, I heard her," Gerry replied, "and, whatever you may say, Mella, I shall have to make a pretence of playing."

"No, Gerry, no! How can you?"

Gerry put his cue back in the rack, then he said:

"You are thinking it is no use and we ought not to be here."

"It would be fascinating if I were not so worried," Carmella answered.

"I know," Gerry said, "and I never slept a wink last night, wondering how we could find that damned safe, and if we do, how we can get into it."

He yawned as he spoke, and Carmella said:

"It is really quite late, I suppose we could go to bed?"

"I do not see why not," Gerry replied. "That is where Sir Robert has gone."

"To bed? But Dolly said they were going to the Conservatory."

She paused, and as Gerry did not answer, she said:

"You do not mean . . . you do not think . . . ?"

Gerry sighed, then he took her hand.

"Now listen, Mella, you know you should not be here, and Mama would be shocked because you are so young that you are mixing with these people, even though they are important. What you have to do is not to think about them, but just be nice to them, and try to enjoy yourself."

"It seems... strange," Carmella said, "that they can be... in love with somebody other than their... husbands or wives and... no one is... shocked."

"It would shock people like Mama—if they knew about it!" Gerry said, as if he were trying to explain it. "But as long as there is no scandal, as long as the newspapers do not get hold of it and nobody talks, there is no reason why people should not enjoy themselves, even if they are married."

"But... I am sure it is wrong!"

Her brother did not answer, and after a moment she said:

"I am sorry... I am not criticising... but if we could go to bed... that is what I would like to do."

"I have already been told that one does what one likes in this house," Gerry said, "and quite frankly, I am dead tired."

Carmella could understand how worried he was, but she also felt it was impossible to sleep when there was so much on their minds, especially when she had to pretend to be somebody else.

They walked from the Billiard-Room into the hall and as they started to ascend the Grand Staircase, they saw ahead of them another couple.

Carmella was just about to say: "We are not the only people going to bed!" when she realised it was Lady Brooke and Lord Charles Beresford.

Because Lady Brooke had been kind to her, she did not want to think that she was behaving, as it seemed to her, immorally, or remember that she had read somewhere, when Lord Charles's brilliant exploits were described, that he had a wife.

"I will not . . . think about it, I will . . . not!" she told herself, and without speaking to Gerry hurried along the corridor to her bedroom.

He caught up with her as she opened her door and she said:

"Goodnight, Gerry, and try to sleep. It is no use worrying. We have just got to hope and pray that things will come right."

He kissed her on the cheek, and without saying anything went along the corridor to his own room.

Carmella rang the bell as Jeanne had told her, and the maid appeared in a few minutes to say:

"You are early, M'Lady. I was expecting you be much later than this."

"I am tired, Jeanne," Carmella said, "and His Lordship is tired too."

"No one in the house is surprised you go to bed," Jeanne said. "Ze servants all saying after dinner you prettiest lady Milord Marquis ever had here!"

"Did they really say that?" Carmella asked.

"They did, an' I agree! You verry beautiful!" Jeanne replied with what Carmella thought was pride, as if she were responsible for it.

She had just stepped out of her gown when there was a knock on the door and Jeanne went to answer it.

She came back with a riding-habit, boots, and a small bowler-hat.

"That Lady Brooke's maid," she explained, "she say

'Er Ladyship think you need them."

"I do indeed!" Carmella said. "And now I shall be able to ride! Oh, Jeanne, it is so exciting for me!"

"Plenty horses here," Jeanne said, "plenty food, plenty money! *Très heureux* for people who have it!"

She sounded envious, but Carmella was thinking that however upsetting tomorrow might be in other ways, at least she would have the wonderful experience of riding what she was sure would be superb, outstanding horses.

She had loved riding with her father, but as the years went by, he had never been able to afford the best horses.

When they went out hunting, Carmella would often feel envious of women who did not ride as well as she did but were mounted on outstanding animals, while she had to make do with inferior ones.

Because she was so excited, she went to bed thinking that when tomorrow came she would try to ride for as long and as often as she possible could.

She was sure when she talked to him about it, Gerry would feel the same.

She fell asleep thinking that however many lies they might have to tell and however frightened she might be, it was almost worth it.

Carmella awoke from a dreamless sleep to realise that the sun was shining through the sides of the curtains, but when she looked at the clock she saw that it was only 6:30 A.M.

Jeanne had told her that breakfast was not served until nine at the earliest, but she felt it was impossible to lie in bed an hour and a half before she could get up.

She therefore pulled back the curtains and saw the

sunshine flooding the Park, and there was a soft mist moving off the lake.

It was so lovely that she felt she must show it to Gerry.

It suddenly struck her after all the Marquis had said that there was no reason why they should not go riding.

She opened the communicating door through which Gerry had come to her last night.

She found herself in a pretty *boudoir* beautifully furnished and decorated with a number of vases of hot-house flowers from what she knew must be the Marquis's greenhouses.

She walked across the room and softly, because she did not wish to disturb him, opened the door which she was sure led into Gerry's bedroom.

As she suspected, he was still asleep, and she tip-toed beside the bed to look down at her brother.

He looked very young and, she thought, very good-looking.

At the same time, she knew, even in his sleep, there was still a worried expression on his face and a little frown between his eye-brows.

Then she saw that the bed was untidy, as if he had been tossing about before he finally went to sleep.

"I will not waken him," she decided, and tip-toed back the way she had come, closing the door quietly behind her.

Then she knew that Gerry or no Gerry, she would take the opportunity while it was there, waiting for her.

Lady Brooke had been right in thinking that they were about the same size, although she was, in fact, a little taller than Her Ladyship, but the habit fitted her almost as if it had been made for her.

In fact, she wished it had been, as it was by Busbine, the best habit-maker in London.

Because she had always dressed herself neatly to go out hunting, she had no difficulty in tying her stock, then arranging her hair so that it was tidy under the small bowler-hat.

It was only a quarter-past-seven when she went from her bedroom down the stairs to ask a sleepy footman, who looked at her in surprise, the way to the stables.

"Oi'll tell 'em you want a 'orse, M'Lady, if you like to wait," he offered.

"I would prefer to go to the stables myself," Carmella answered.

Through the front door the footman pointed to where she could see at the other end of the house there was an archway which he told her led into the stables.

Because she was so excited at what lay ahead, she almost ran across the court-yard and through the archway until she found the cobble-stones of the stable-yard.

Then, as she was hoping to see a groom to tell him what she wanted, out of the stables came a black stallion, bucking and rearing, and being held with some difficulty by two grooms. Behind them came the Marquis.

He looked at her in surprise, and said:

"Good morning, Lady O'Kerry! You are very early!"

Carmella, fearing he was annoyed at her appearance, said quickly:

"You did say I could ride whenever I wished."

"Of course," he answered. "I am only astonished that you are not still asleep, like the rest of my house-party."

"And may I have a horse to ride?"

"Of course you may! Come and choose which one you would like."

He ignored the prancing stallion which he left in the charge of the two boys, and went back into the stables, where Carmella followed him.

The stables were, as she expected, finer than any she had ever seen, as she was certain would be the animals occupying them.

Eagerly, forgetting everything for the moment in her excitement at the thought of riding a horse that was really outstanding, she peeped into the first two stalls, then the third, then the fourth, then passed on to the fifth.

It contained a horse that was not unlike the stallion which she knew the Marquis intended to rid.

As she stood looking at it, he said:

"I warn you, 'Flycatcher' can be very obstreperous, and he pulls rather hard."

"Please, may I ride him?"

"You are quite certain you can manage him?"

"I shall be very ashamed if I say 'yes,' and he proves me wrong!"

The Marquis smiled.

"Very well."

He gave the order and Flycatcher was quickly saddled and taken into the yard.

Carmella expected he would be taken to the mounting-block, but instead the Marquis lifted her into the saddle, then mounting his own stallion, as if he knew he must lead the way, went ahead.

Because the stallion was still showing off a little, Carmella's horse did the same.

She bent forward to pat him and talk to him in a low voice, and by the time the Marquis was halfway down the drive toward the lake, Flycatcher appeared to have settled down.

When he got to the other side of the bridge over the lake, the Marquis reined in his horse and waited for Carmella to catch up with him.

"Are you all right?" he asked.

"I have never been so happy!" she replied.

The Marquis looked at her as if he thought she was exaggerating her feelings just to impress him, but once again she was talking to Flycatcher and the horse was listening to her, twitching his ears as he did so.

"Come along," the Marquis said. "I think we should gallop some of the devil out of them, and sweep away the cobwebs in our own brains at the same time!"

Carmella wanted to say that as far as she was concerned, she had no cobwebs.

Then she remembered how worried and anxious she was and thought that, in fact, was more insidious and very much harder to get rid of than what the Marquis was talking about.

She followed him across the Park and realised he was going slowly so as to avoid the rabbit-holes and the lower branches of the trees.

Then on the other side she saw they had come to a flat piece of land which she realized made a perfect place for a Gallop.

She did not wait for the Marquis to give her permission, but started off immediately and there was no doubt that Flycatcher intended to race the Marquis's stallion and to win.

They must have galloped for nearly a mile before the

Marquis drew in his horse, and Carmella realised she was meant to do the same.

They had been riding neck-and-neck, but she knew without being told that, if the Marquis had exerted himself, he could have made his stallion beat Flycatcher.

As they came down the Gallop at first a trot, then a walk, Carmella said:

"That was wonderful! I have never ridden a better horse than Flycatcher, but I would really love the opportunity of riding your stallion."

She spoke without thinking, and feared as she finished the sentence that it might sound rather presumptuous, but the Marquis smiled and said:

"I think you would find him rather hard to hold, though may I say, Lady O'Kerry, I am very impressed by the way you manage Flycatcher!"

As he finished speaking, he gave a laugh and as Carmella looked at him in surprise he said:

"I was just thinking—it is often frail, fragile little women, who look as though a puff of wind would blow them away, who can handle a horse better than the more obvious Amazon!"

"As I think that must be a compliment," Carmella said, "thank you! My father always said I was a good rider, but I thought he might be prejudiced."

"What does Bramforde think about it?" the Marquis enquired.

"Gerry... Gerald has ridden since he could crawl!" Carmella said. "So he is as happy as I am when he has a decent horse to ride."

She spoke without thinking and only realised what she had said when the Marquis remarked:

"Then you have known Bramforde for a long time! I thought perhaps you had just met."

"No, we both lived in Gloucestershire," Carmella said, thinking that was a good explanation.

"And, of course, you are very much in love with him!"

The Marquis spoke in a cynical voice which made it difficult for a moment for Carmella to realise exactly what he was saying.

Having no idea what to answer, she did not reply.

She just looked ahead of them as they moved down from the Gallop towards a field which had a twisting stream bordered by willow trees running through it.

"I have a feeling you think I am being impertinent," the Marquis said after what seemed to Carmella a long pause.

Then he added:

"If he is so keen on riding, why did Bramforde not come with you this morning?"

Because it was a relief to get away from the subject of love, Carmella answered:

"I peeped in at him and he was fast asleep. He was very tired last night after he had finished playing Billiards, and I thought it would be a mistake to wake him, even though I know he would love to go riding."

She had no idea that the Marquis raised his eyebrows as if in surprise before he said:

"I think that was very considerate of you."

Carmella laughed.

"I hope Gerry thinks so. I have a feeling when he realises I have been riding a horse as magnificent as Flycatcher he will think I have 'stolen a march' on him!"

"Or perhaps he might be jealous," the Marquis remarked.

Carmella looked at him in surprise, and for a moment did not realise what he was suggesting. Then she said quickly:

"I do not think it would be a question of jealousy where you are concerned, My Lord, but envy. You have everything that any man could possible want, and I suppose it is difficult not to feel that the 'crumbs from the rich man's table' are not particularly satisfying."

Then because she felt he did not understand or perhaps that it was wrong for her to criticise, Carmella urged Flycatcher forward, and sped off, leaving the Marquis to take some minutes to catch up with her.

As he did so he said:

"I see, Lady O'Kerry, you are very experienced in evading difficult questions. Are you as adroit when it comes to a situation which is also difficult?"

"I do not know what you mean," Carmella replied, then added quickly: "I am sorry if I was rude. I did not mean to be."

"You were not in the least rude," the Marquis replied, "only frank and truthful. And may I say, in all sincerity, that it is something I like to hear, because it seldom happens."

Carmella thought this over before she said:

"You mean, because you are so important and so frightening that people tell you what they think you want to hear, rather than what they really think?"

"So you think I am frightening?" the Marquis asked.

Carmella gave a little laugh.

"Of course you are! You must be aware of that!"

"Are you frightened of me?"

"I was very, very frightened before I arrived and when I first met you... but you were very kind last night when I asked you not to let Gerry play cards... and you have been so kind to me this morning... so now I feel better!"

She spoke, the Marquis thought, almost in a childlike way.

At the same time, he was aware that only somebody with a quick, alert and perhaps astute brain could have thought out the situation so clearly.

"Then may I say, Lady O'Kerry," he replied, "that I hope I never give you reason to be frightened of me in the future."

"I hope not too!" Carmella said fervently.

As she spoke, she remembered the Bramforde Necklace, and why they were here, and knew that from that point of view, if no other, the Marquis was terrifying!

chapter five

WHEN Carmella and the Marquis arrived back at the Hall, it was just after nine o'clock, and as they walked up the steps towards the front door she said a little nervously:

"Shall I . . . change before breakfast?"

"I am sure you are hungry," the Marquis answered, "so I should come in exactly as you are, which is what I intend to do myself."

Having put her gloves and whip down on a chair, Carmella hesitated a moment, then took off the small bowler-hat which Lady Brooke had lent her.

She tidied her hair in a looking-glass, then without spending much time on it went into the Breakfast-Room with the Marquis.

It was not as large or impressive as the Dining-Room, but the sunshine was coming in through the windows, and she saw, as she had expected, a sideboard laden with silver *entrée* dishes, each with a candle underneath it to keep the food warm.

To her surprise there was no one else there, and the Marquis walking across the room to inspect the dishes said:

"I have a feeling that my other guests will be late, and you and I will eat alone."

"I thought, as it was Friday night, that everybody would go to bed early," Carmella replied. "The ladies were all talking about the Balls they attended last week, and how they felt exhausted."

"And which Ball did you go to?" the Marquis asked.

Carmella laughed.

"I have never been to a Ball!"

She spoke as herself without thinking, and when she saw the surprise on his face, she said quickly:

"You know I have been in mourning for a year."

"But, before that, surely your husband took you to a Ball, even though you lived in the country?"

Carmella shook her head and said quickly to avoid answering any further questions:

"There are so many dishes that I cannot choose which looks the nicest!"

"Then why not try each one?" the Marquis suggested. "But I am well aware, Lady O'Kerry, that once again you are evading my question."

Carmella was afraid that she might blush, and she therefore turned her head away from him and helped herself from one of the *entrée* dishes.

As she walked back to the table, which was laid for a large number, she hesitated but thought it would seem strange if she did not sit down next to the Marquis.

She hoped, as she did so, she was not taking Lady Sybil's place, or one of his more important guests.

The Marquis helped himself from the sideboard, then sat himself down, saying as he did so:

"Are you not worried that Bramforde is still sleeping? Perhaps when he wakes he will be asking what has happened to you."

"Gerry will not worry about me," Carmella answered, "and if he thinks about it at all, he will be sure I have gone riding."

Again she did not see the surprise in the Marquis's eyes. He did not say anything, but merely helped her and himself to coffee which stood on a tray in front of him.

"Tell me what you are entering in the Gold Cup at Ascot this year?" Carmella begged, feeling that horses would be a safe topic of conversation.

She was listening intently to what the Marquis was saying, when a number of male guests came into the room, and after that there was no question of her talking to the Marquis alone.

Later in the day she realised that Lady Sybil was being deliberately rude to her.

While at first she was surprised, she then realised it was because she had been riding early in the morning with the Marquis.

"You must be very tough to get up so early, Lady O'Kerry!" she said in a caustic voice which made Carmella feel uncomfortable. "I am afraid I have never been one of those hard-hunting horsey sort of women who are usually spattered in mud and smell of the stables!"

Several women laughed at what she said, and one of them remarked:

"No one could accuse you of that, Sybil, but you are tough in other ways which we would not like to mention!"

"I am not afraid to admit I am tough when somebody tries to take something of mine away from me," Lady Sybil replied. "Then I am prepared to fight with every weapon available."

As it was quite obvious what she was insinuating,

Carmella got up from where she was sitting and moved across the room.

She wished there were someone she could talk to without it appearing obvious she was upset by the way Lady Sybil was attacking her.

Gerry had disappeared for the moment, and there seemed to be nobody in the room who was in the least interested in her.

Then Lady Brooke came to the rescue.

"Come and talk to me, Lady O'Kerry," she said. "I am sure you find the Marquis's horses as delightful as I do, and I hear we are all going riding after luncheon."

"I am so grateful to you for lending me your habit," Carmella said in a low voice, hoping Lady Sybil would not overhear, "and it was wonderful riding a better horse than I have ever been able to ride before."

"One day you must come and stay with me at Easton," Lady Brooke said. "Then I will show you my stables. I shall be very disappointed if you do not think they rival if not excel, the Marquis's!"

"What are you saying about me?" a voice asked.

With a start Carmella realised that the Marquis had come into the room while they were talking, and she had not noticed him.

"I was telling Lady O'Kerry that I hope my horses will seem to her as good as she thinks yours are," Daisy Brooke said with a smile, "but I shall feel more sure of myself after I have seen the new ones you promised to show me."

"Why do we not go and look at them now?" the Marquis suggested.

"Oh, and that reminds me," Daisy Brooke said.

"When you have finished showing me your horses, I want to see your new safe."

He looked surprised and Lady Brooke went on:

"You told Brookie you had one of the new Combination safes, which are much more effective than the old ones, and because Brookie is always worried about my jewels, I told him that while I was here I would see what yours is like and decide if we could install one at Easton."

"I shall be delighted to show it to you," the Marquis said, "and we will go and look at it after tea."

Carmella drew in her breath and with an effort she managed to say:

"May I see it too? I have heard about Combination safes, but have never had a chance of seeing one."

"We will look at it together," Lady Brooke said, "and while we are about it, we will make Tyrone show us the Ingleton tiaras."

She laughed as she said:

"He has always maintained they are better than mine, but as he refuses to take a wife and keeps them all to himself, I am never quite certain whether he is boasting or telling the truth."

"You shall see the family jewels," the Marquis said good-humouredly, "and, let me add, I intend to leave them in the safe for many years yet."

"Oh, Tyrone, how can you be so obstinate?" Lady Brooke exclaimed. "I know you will have to marry sometime and have an heir, for if you do not, that terrible, boring uncle of yours will come into the title! I cannot bear to think what he would do to this beautiful house, which is perfect in every way."

"Now you are flattering me," the Marquis said, "but

even to please you, Daisy, I am not going to be hurried up the aisle."

"I will make sure of that!" Lady Sybil said.

She had crossed the room as the Marquis was talking, drawn to him as if he were a magnet, and now she slipped her arm through his and looked up at him from under her eye-lashes.

"We are very happy as we are," she said, "and Tyrone, as he quite rightly says, must keep his diamonds in the safe."

The Marquis disentangled himself from Lady Sybil's grasp and put out his hand toward Lady Brooke.

"Come and see my horses," he said. "I value your opinion, Daisy, and I want to show them off to you."

"How can I resist such an invitation." Lady Brooke smiled.

She put her hand into his and they walked towards the door, leaving Lady Sybil looking after them with her lips pressed tightly together.

Then as if she had to vent her rage on somebody, she said to Carmella:

"I think it is an Irish characteristic to be pushy, Lady O'Kerry, and I cannot understand why you are not running after the Marquis now, in case he gets away from you!"

The words seemed to end in a kind of snarl, and without waiting for Carmella to reply she walked away.

It was only a short time before luncheon, but Carmella feeling shaken went up to her bedroom.

Jeanne was not there, and she thought it was a relief because the maid would continue scolding her for going out riding without telling her, and of course without her face made up as it should have been.

"I thought it was too early to wake you," Carmella had explained a little lamely.

"*M'mselle* tell me watch over you," Jeanne said, "and without me your face look young, very young! Not like lady who lose husband."

"I . . . I am sorry," Carmella said humbly. "I will not forget again."

She told herself that although she had ridden with the Marquis and had breakfast with him, it was very unlikely he had noticed that she looked any different from what she had last night.

Jeanne however scolded her all the time she was changing into one of the pretty day-gowns which *Mademoiselle* Yvonne had lent her, arranging her hair, making up her eyes and her lips as she had done yesterday.

"Now you are *chic*, and more experienced," she said as she finished. "But look a little bored, M'Lady, *les grandes dames sont toujours blasées*."

Carmella laughed.

"It is very difficult to be blasé here, where everything is so exquisite and exciting!"

Then she hurried down the stairs, afraid of missing anything, because she knew she would never see such luxury, or be in such beautiful surroundings again.

After luncheon, which was a light-hearted and amusing meal despite the fact that Lady Sybil appeared to be sulking and saying spiteful things to everybody around her, they all went riding.

The ladies having changed surprisingly quickly, the whole house-party rode off like a cavalcade on the Marquis's horses towards the race-course he had erected about a mile from the house.

It was on the opposite side of the Park from where

they had ridden that morning, and Carmella, who had never seen a private race-course, was thrilled.

It was larger than she expected, and the jumps were higher, but she knew she could manage them if she had the chance.

The Marquis was once again paying a lot of attention to Lady Brooke, but now Lord Charles was with them, and although he rode well, as a sailor he was not in the same category as the Marquis or indeed Gerry.

Carmella had only to look at her brother to see he was in his element and had forgotten for the moment his worry over money or the necklace.

He was thinking only of the horse he was riding, which gave him the same pleasure as she had felt this morning, when she was on Flycatcher.

Because he was so excited, he forgot that he should be in attendance on Carmella. He was in fact chatting animatedly to several men and was surprised when Lady Sybil rode up and began to talk to him in what seemed a very flattering manner.

As he was not aware that she was annoyed with Carmella and also with Lady Brooke, who she thought was monopolising the Marquis, he was delighted at her attention.

Realising what was expected of him, he paid her a number of compliments which were distinctly flirtatious.

In return she flattered him cleverly in a manner at which she was an expert.

Sybil Greeson was actually only just twenty-six, but she had learnt in the last years how to attract a man, and could make him feel very masculine and desirable just by the way she looked at him.

She kept Gerry by her side until the Marquis said that the gentlemen would compete with one another over the jumps, but he thought they would be too high for the ladies.

"You insult us!" Lady Brooke said. "I, personally, have every intention of jumping every fence just to show that you are wrong!"

She saw Carmella was listening and said:

"Come along, Lady O'Kerry, I am sure you can help me show these gentlemen that we are as good as they are, if not better!"

Before Carmella could answer, she rode ahead and took the first fence in style with a foot to spare, and Carmella followed her.

She was aware as she set off that the Marquis was saying.

"No, Lady O'Kerry, I think it is a mistake for you."

Then she was gone.

She was riding a horse that was even more spirited than Flycatcher, and he took her over the first fence in a manner which told her the Marquis's fears were unfounded.

Lady Brooke was still ahead, and as they went down the race-course, taking every fence with an expertise which no one could fault, the Marquis stopped anyone from following them.

The party watched until half-way round Carmella deliberately made her horse pass Lady Brooke's.

It was what he was only too willing to do, being used to racing the Marquis's other horses when they were training, and the two horses took the next fence together with only a few inches between them.

Then without any challenge having been made, Carmella and Lady Brooke were both riding as hard as they could, each woman determined to beat the other.

At the last fence once again it would have been difficult to say who was ahead.

Then, almost as if she did it by sheer will-power, Carmella passed the Marquis, who was standing at the winning-post, half a length in front of Lady Brooke.

There were cries of "Bravo!" and Carmella turned her horse round to go back to where everybody had been watching.

Then Daisy Brooke, with her usual sweetness said, as she drew up to her:

"You are a magnificent rider, Lady O'Kerry, but another time I will race you on one of my horses!"

"I hope there will be another time," Carmella answered, and Lady Brooke said lightly:

"I shall insist that there will be!"

They rode up to the Marquis and Lady Brooke, obviously teasing him, said:

"Next time, Tyrone, you will have to give me a better horse than this! The poor thing is really too old and too slow for me!"

Everybody laughed because they knew it was a joke, and the Marquis said:

"You both rode magnificently, as you are well aware, and now the rest of us are going to show you how to do it."

Most of the women, including Lady Sybil, said they would rather not risk the jumps, and after the men had performed very ably although Carmella thought the Marquis outrode them all, they went back to the house by a different route.

Lady Sybil was still monopolising Gerald, and Carmella did not get a chance to tell him the exciting news that she was actually going to be shown the safe.

In fact, it was only when she went up to change before tea that she sent Jeanne to see if he was in his bedroom.

When she learned that he was she hurried across the *boudoir*.

He was alone, without a valet with him, and as she shut the door she said:

"I have something to tell you!"

"I have never enjoyed an afternoon more!" Gerry exclaimed. "Oh, Mella, why can I not have a house and horses like that? I was thinking as I was riding round how easy it could be to make a race-course at home."

"I know, dearest," Carmella replied, "but it is impossible, and what we have to think about now is the thousand pounds you owe the Marquis."

"Damn him!" Gerry exploded angrily. "Why does he have so much, and we have nothing? It is not fair!"

He spoke as if he were a little boy deprived of some special toy, and Carmella put her arm around his shoulders and said:

"It is no use, dearest, you have to face facts, and I came to tell you that I am going with Lady Brooke after tea to see the safe!"

Gerry's attention was instantly diverted.

"How have you managed that?"

Carmella told him what Lady Brooke had said and the Marquis's promise to show them the safe and the Ingleton jewels.

"The necklace will be there," he said. "Look to see where it is, if you can, and if it is a Combination safe, as you say it is, for God's sake try to follow the combination as he unlocks it."

"You mean... you are expecting... me to open it later?" Carmella asked in a frightened voice.

"I will come with you," Gerry said, "but I shall not be much use unless you know the formula of the Combination."

"Oh, Gerry, it is so frightening."

"I know, I know!" he agreed. "But we have to think of Mama, and if the necklace is discovered to be false, what will everybody say about her selling the real sapphires?"

Carmella thought he should have thought of that when he gambled it away, but she did not say anything.

When Jeanne had helped her change her gown and done her hair, she went downstairs feeling frightened, at the same time convinced that however optimistic Gerry might be, she was certain to fail him.

There was tea in the Orangery, where the orange trees which had come from Spain were covered with fruit which although not yet ripe was already slightly golden.

It was something Carmella had never seen before. She was quite fascinated by the flowers which grew in the Orangery, although she had heard somebody say that the conservatory was even more impressive.

As she looked at the azaleas which she was told the Marquis had brought from India, and the orchids which had come from many parts of the world, she thought it was understandable that Gerry should be envious and perhaps every other man in the house-party felt the same.

It seemed extraordinary that as he had so much, the Marquis should look cynical and, when he was not smiling, bored.

"How could anybody be bored with all this?" she asked beneath her breath and gave a little start as she found the Marquis standing beside her.

"What are you thinking about so intently, Lady O'Kerry?" he asked.

"I was...admiring your...orchids," she replied a little hesitatingly.

"And what else were you thinking?"

She thought it was perceptive of him to know she had been thinking of anything else.

Then because it seemed quite natural to tell him the truth, she replied:

"I was...wondering how with all this...you could possibly be...bored."

"Is that what you think I am?" the Marquis asked sharply.

"It is how you look sometimes," Carmella said, "and also—"

She stopped and the Marquis said:

"Finish the sentance."

"I am being rude," Carmella answered, "but you did ask me."

"And I want an answer."

"Very well," she said a little defiantly. "You look contemptuous and cynical instead of happy, as you should be. Why are you not...happy?"

She found to her own surprise the words almost tumbling out of her mouth.

The Marquis looked at her before he said:

"Perhaps one day I will give you an answer, but now

I am taking Lady Brooke to see the Ingleton diamonds, and you said you wished to come too."

"Yes . . . of course," Carmella agreed.

At the same time her heart gave a frightened leap as she was so sure that what she would see would only make Gerry's plan seem even more difficult than it had before.

Lady Brooke was waiting for them at the other end of the Orangery.

As Carmella joined her she was aware that Gerry was sitting beside Lady Sybil, who was talking to him in an intimate fashion.

And as they passed, she gave the Marquis a provocative, defiant look, as if to show she was scoring over him.

He did not however appear to notice, and when they joined Lady Brooke, they walked down the long passage and through the hall and then into another wing of the house.

"Where do you keep your safe?" Daisy Brooke asked curiously. "I keep mine in my bedroom."

"Mine is far too big for that," the Marquis replied, "and I therefore house it in my secretary's room so that he has his eye on it for the best part of the day."

"And at night?" Lady Brooke asked.

"At night two night watchmen go round the house at hourly intervals and they look at the safe every time they pass my secretary's office."

"That sounds very sensible," Daisy Brooke said. "But where a woman is concerned, her diamonds would be continually going up and down the stairs, and I think they are better in my bedroom, as you may find when you marry."

"Stop match-making, Daisy!" the Marquis said in an amused tone. "If you think I am going to marry one of those tiresome débutantes who are paraded in front of me at the Spring Sales, then you can think again!"

Lady Brooke gave a little chuckle of laughter.

"The Spring Sales!" she said. "Is that what you call the Balls at the beginning of the Season?"

"I think it is an apt name for them," the Marquis said. "Every mother is ready to sell her daughter to the highest title she can obtain, and I am quite a long way up the ladder!"

He spoke with such a note of contempt in his voice that Carmella longed to say that it spoilt him to feel like that.

Then suddenly as he looked at her, she was aware that he knew what she was thinking and she blushed.

The secretary's room was large, filled with filing-cabinets and dispatch-boxes, while the walls were covered with maps of the estate.

Against one wall stood a very large safe, far larger than Carmella had expected.

Daisy Brooke gave a cry of delight as she exclaimed:

"So that is a Combination safe! How exciting! Do show me how it works!"

"That is just what I intend to do," the Marquis said good-humouredly.

He went to the safe, then said as if he were talking to himself:

"Now, what did Maynard tell me was the new combination? We change it every month or so. Oh, I remember—he has had a classical education and he therefore uses the gods and goddesses who have four-letter names. This month it is *JUNO*."

"Show me how it works," Daisy Brooke begged.

The Marquis bent down and turned the combination lock round and round until it stopped in turn at the four letters he had mentioned, then the door was open and Carmella saw that everything inside it was arranged neatly on steel shelves.

It was all wrapped either in tissue-paper or in baize bags.

"Do you keep the silver in here?" Lady Brooke asked.

"No, there is not enough room for it," the Marquis explained. "It is kept in another safe, which I must soon replace, as it is an old-fashioned key type, and is in the Pantry."

As if he thought his listeners might think it a risk, he added:

"One of the footmen always sleeps in the Pantry, which means it is more or less guarded by day and by night."

Daisy Brooke smiled and said:

"We have just the same arrangement, and when things are stolen from other houses, I always think it is the owner's fault."

"Then I hope you will not think that I am inefficient," the Marquis said.

As he spoke he put out his hand towards the second shelf down in the safe and drew from the back of it a large case covered in red leather.

Emblazoned on it was the Marquis's crest, and when he opened the case, Carmella saw it contained the most magnificent diamond tiara she had ever dreamt of seeing.

"This is the one my mother always wore at the

Opening of Parliament," the Marquis said.

As Daisy Brooke lifted the tiara out of its velvet-lined box she said:

"It is beautiful, Tyrone, larger than mine, and the stones are bigger."

"My grandfather brought a great number of diamonds back from Africa," the Marquis explained, "and I have always been told that they are blue-white. I remember as a little boy thinking, if my mother came to say goodnight to me when she was wearing it, she looked like a Fairy Queen."

"That is how every mother should look to her children," Daisy Brooke said quietly. "But how can you bear to have anything as beautiful as this shut away in a safe instead of seeing it on some lovely woman's head?"

There was silence before the Marquis said:

"I have always sworn that only my wife shall wear this tiara, when and if I have one."

"Oh, dear!" Daisy Brooke exclaimed. "What a pity I am already married! Otherwise, Tyrone dear, I might even marry you for your jewels."

As she spoke in her teasing voice, Carmella was aware that the Marquis's lips were set in a tight line, and his eyes seemed suddenly dark.

Then as if he controlled himself with an effort he took the tiara from Daisy Brooke's hand, put it back in its box, and set it on the shelf of the safe from which it had come.

Then he opened case after case, one of them containing a necklace with five rows of diamonds, another a smaller tiara, to be worn on less important occasions than the Opening of Parliament.

There were bracelets for each wrist, and a diamond

ring that seemed in its depth and brightness to flash light as if it was a star as the Marquis held it in his hand.

Daisy Brooke and, of course, Carmella admired everything.

Then the Marquis showed them sets of other stones which his mother and grandmother had collected. There were tiaras, necklaces, bracelets, and earrings of every imaginable stone.

There was a sapphire set, a pearl set, and last of all an emerald set which had come from India which Daisy Brooke said was unique and far excelled anything anyone in Society possessed, including the Princess of Wales.

Then as they reached the fourth shelf the Marquis hesitated for a moment and Carmella perceptively knew, although he did not say so, that he was thinking of the Bramforde Necklace and she was sure that was where it had been put.

Just for a moment she wondered if she might ask him to show it to her so that she would know exactly where to find it.

Then she told herself it would be a very foolish thing to do, and it was important that Lady Broke should not know he had won it from Gerry.

As if the Marquis thought the same thing, he looked at Carmella, then shut the safe, saying as he did so:

"That, I may say, is the end of the performance! I hope you have enjoyed it!"

"I have never seen such wonderful jewels," Daisy Brooke enthused, "and, Tyrone, you must show them to Princess Alexandra the next time she comes to Ingleton. I know she would be thrilled, and they are better than anything in the Royal collection!"

"That is what I would like to think," the Marquis replied.

He shut the door, and now he was setting the combination on the safe, and, following the movements of his hands, Carmella knew that she could quite easily copy him.

Then she wondered wryly how she could ever stoop to steal anything, even a necklace which belonged to her mother.

Because the idea perturbed her, she walked away to stand looking up with unseeing eyes at one of the maps on the wall.

'Supposing I tell the Marquis the truth?' she thought. 'What would he say? What would he do?'

Then she told herself that to do so would be to betray Gerry.

What was more, she would have to confess she was not Lady O'Kerry, but as his sister far more deeply concerned with Gerry's wild action in throwing away the necklace, and at the same time losing a thousand pounds.

She was thinking how little a thousand pounds would mean to the Marquis, when she heard him say:

"I am going to take you back now, and I expect you both want to rest before dinner."

"I think that is a good idea, after all that hard riding," Daisy Brooke laughed, "and I am sure you have an exciting evening planned for us."

"I hope you will find it exciting," the Marquis said. "I have a number of people coming to dinner, and I have engaged an Orchestra to play afterwards in the Ballroom, although naturally there will be other amusements for those who want them."

"It sounds delightful!" Daisy Brooke exclaimed. "You know, Tyrone, you are superlative as a host, as well as at everything else."

"I try to be," the Marquis said, "but Lady O'Kerry persists in looking worried, and I am afraid I am failing where she is concerned."

Carmella realised that Lady Brooke looked at her in surprise, and she could not help the colour coming into her face as she said:

"Oh, no! That is not true! I have never enjoyed anything more than I have enjoyed today, and thank you for showing me your beautiful family jewels."

She tried to speak spontaneously, but she had the feeling that the Marquis was looking at her once again in that deep, penetrating way.

She suspected he was reading her thoughts as she had been able to read his, and knew the truth.

Then she told herself she was being ridiculous and managed with a superhuman effort to talk normally as they walked back towards the Hall.

When they reached the staircase, Lady Brooke said:

"Thank you, Tyrone, dear, for a unique entertainment which I greatly enjoyed! Now I am going to find Charles and tell him I am going to rest."

She moved away in the direction of the Orangery, and Carmella said:

"I want to thank you, too, before I go upstairs."

"I wish you would tell me what is worrying you," the Marquis said.

"I cannot think why you should... say that I am... worried," Carmella replied hesitatingly.

"Shall I say your eyes are very expressive? And ever since you arrived, my instinct has told me that you are different from what you appear to be."

Carmella looked at him in astonishment. Then because she suddenly felt embarrassed she said:

"Now you are... imagining things which are not... true, and you are... frightening me again, which... you promised not to do."

"I am trying not to frighten you," the Marquis said, "but as you will not let me help you, I find it extraordinarily frustrating."

Because what he said made her more frightened than ever that he might guess her secret, Carmella turned away.

She had one foot on the bottom step of the staircase and her hand was on the bannister when the Marquis said:

"If you trust me, you will find me a very good friend, and I want to help you."

Again Carmella had an impulse to tell him everything, but she knew it was something she must not do.

Gerry would never forgive her, for she was well aware that a gambling debt was a debt of honour and had to be paid, although how they were to do so she had not the slightest idea.

Just for a moment her eyes were held by his, and she felt as if the Marquis was drawing her with a strange power and magnetism she could not understand, but could feel.

Then with a sigh that was almost like the cry of a small animal caught in a trap, she ran away from him up the stairs as quickly as she could.

Reaching the landing, she sped along the corridor to her own room, and only when she had shut the door behind her was she aware that her heart was thumping in a very strange way in her breast.

Her breath was coming quickly from between her lips, but it was not only because she had hurried, but because of the feelings the Marquis had evoked in her.

Then because the realisation was so overwhelming and because it was something she could not put into words, she wanted to run away from herself

The Marquis stood looking after Carmella in bewilderment when she had left him, then slowly he walked back to the Orangery.

For the rest of the evening he found himself preoccupied with thinking about the strange expression in her eyes, and the little cry that seemed to him one of despair as well as fear, when she had run away from him.

When she came down for dinner escorted by Gerald, the Marquis told himself he was being ridiculous.

There was nothing wrong except that for some reason Lady O'Kerry seemed much younger, much less sure of herself than he would have expected, considering she was a widow and must, from what had been said, be at least twenty-three or -four years old.

At dinner, seated between two very lovely and important ladies from another house-party, although they flirted agreeably with him, he found himself continually watching Carmella.

She was sitting farther down the table with Gerald on one side of her and Sir Robert on the other.

He thought that, although she looked exceedingly beautiful and was wearing a very attractive and obviously expensive necklace, she looked pale.

He imagined, although he could not be sure, that there was still an expression of fear in her eyes.

"What has Bramforde been up to?" he asked himself, and could not believe that Carmella was upset simply because Lady Sybil was making him behave in a somewhat outrageous fashion.

It was unusual for the Marquis to be worrying himself over a woman, and certainly not one in whom he was not personally interested.

In that case he usually thought more of his own feelings than of hers.

His eyes went back to the necklace that Carmella was wearing, and he told himself cynically that she had not mentioned it this afternoon, when she and Daisy were admiring his jewels.

She was obviously, like all the women he knew, starting to collect the baubles which meant so much to them personally.

They were like, he thought, the African women who hoarded their bangles and the Indians the little diamonds they set in their noses.

"All women are the same!" he told himself bitterly, yet found it impossible not to think that Lady O'Kerry was different from all the other ladies in the party.

Because he was used to analysing people, usually to their disadvantage, he asked himself what was different about her.

He found it hard to find an answer.

She was beautiful, but so was every other woman in the room.

She certainly did not seem to understand how to be flirtatious or provocative.

But that was obviously because, as she had told him, she had lived in the country, and he suspected she had not therefore met many men.

Then it suddenly struck him that she behaved in an entirely different way towards him and all the other men in the party from that of any of the other women.

It was not only that she did not flirt; it was as if there was an aura of innocence and purity around her. But that, of course, was impossible, as she had been married.

And yet he could feel it almost as if she vibrated towards him in a way that was unique.

He was so silent that one of the ladies beside him looked at him apprehensively, then asked:

"What's wrong, Tyrone? I have never known you to be so difficult to talk to as you are tonight."

"I must apologise," the Marquis said, "I wanted you to enjoy my party."

"Which I am very eager to do."

She gave him an inviting little glance from under her eye-lashes as she spoke, and there was no doubt from the soft note in her voice what she meant.

'That is the difference!' the Marquis thought to himself.

He knew, almost as if he had received a sudden revelation, that it would be impossible for Carmella to speak like that for the simple reason that she had never been awakened to the fires of passion that women called "love."

He found it an intriguing thought and he wanted to talk to her again.

But when the gentlemen left the Dining-Room, having consumed a large amount of port and brandy, the Orchestra was already playing in the Ball-Room.

The ladies were waiting impatiently for partners, either on the polished floor, or at the green baize tables laid out once again in the Drawing-Room.

The Marquis then had to organise things.

By the time he had got some of the older men seated at the card-tables and ensured that everybody else was dancing, he was aware that Sybil, because she was annoyed with him, was deliberately dancing in a somewhat intimate manner with Gerald Bramforde.

Her eyes met the Marquis's across the dance-floor and he knew she was inciting him to be jealous and hoping he would snatch her away from the young man she had caught by her almost professional wiles.

It was due, the Marquis was aware, to the fact that he had not made love to her last night, simply because he was tired and had suddenly no wish to be involved with Sybil and her exotic charms with which he was all too familiar.

Instead, he had gone to bed alone and had risen early to find to his surprise that Carmella had done the same thing.

Because the servants talked, it had been impossible to keep from Sybil the knowledge that they had ridden together, and he knew her lady's-maid regaled her with all the gossip concerning the house-party.

He thus was aware as soon as Sybil appeared that she was furiously angry that he had been accompanied on his morning ride.

While she had been too experienced to create a scene, he had known that all her behaviour throughout the day had been in retaliation for what she considered an insult to her personally.

Now as he walked from the Ball-Room, aware that Bramforde was dancing with Sybil, there was no sign of Carmella, and he wondered where she could be, knowing he was unlikely to find her with the gamblers.

Almost as if she drew him, he walked to the Picture Gallery which occupied almost entirely the first floor of the West Wing.

He had just recently had it lit by electricity, and lights shone over each picture, while the chandeliers in the centre of the ceiling were not switched on.

It made the Picture Gallery look very attractive, and at the same time very romantic.

When he saw Carmella at the far end, he thought that in her gown of pale green she looked like a nymph that might have risen from the lake, and was neither substantial nor human.

Quietly he moved towards her and found when he reached her that she was gazing up at an exquisite picture of the Virgin and Child which he had bought when he was last in Rome.

It was a picture he had liked so much, that he had paid a large sum of money for it, not because of its intrinsic value, but simply because it appealed to him.

Now as he reached Carmella's side he thought to his amazement that he knew she felt the same about it as he did, and was as moved as he had been when he had first seen it.

She did not turn her head, but as he stood beside her she said quietly:

"It is so beautiful . . . so exquisitely beautiful that one could only . . . describe it in . . . music!"

"That is what I thought when I bought it," the Marquis agreed.

"Did it give you the feeling that it was... speaking to you? Telling you something you must... hear, and yet it is what you know... already if you... listen to your... heart?"

She was speaking in such a low voice that the Marquis was aware she was thinking it out for herself rather than telling him what it meant.

"That is what I felt," he said, "and I knew, as soon as I saw you standing there, that it was what you are feeling too."

She did not move for a moment, then she slowly turned her head, and looked up at him she said:

"If you can feel like that... if you can come here and let this picture talk to you... how can you ever be... cynical or... bored?"

"I am neither of those things at the moment," the Marquis said, "because I am with you!"

He did not mean to say the words, and yet spontaneously they came to his lips.

Any other woman he knew would have moved at once into his arms, but Carmella merely turned again to the picture, saying:

"That is how I would like to be... but perhaps it could only happen if I had... a baby of my own."

She looked at the Christchild as she spoke.

It was then the Marquis realised that was how she did look—like the Madonna—in a strange way.

That was why, the moment he had first seen her, he had thought that she reminded him of somebody, but he could not think who it could be.

He was about to say something of what he was

thinking and feeling, but before he could put it into words, Carmella said in a different voice altogether:

"Why are you here? You should be with your guests. There is nothing... wrong?"

It flashed through her mind that something had happened to Gerry, or perhaps the Marquis had discovered that she was deceiving him.

"There is nothing wrong," he said quietly, "except that I wondered, when everybody else was dancing, what had happened to you."

Carmella gave a little cry. Then she answered:

"No one asked me to dance, and I came away. I am so very glad I did so. Why did you not tell me you had all these wonderful pictures? I could have spent an hour here after seeing your safe!"

"I am sure it was much better for you to rest," the Marquis said, "and there is always tomorrow."

"Yes, of course," Carmella answered, "and thank you for coming to find me, but I think we should... go back."

She spoke a little nervously and because the Marquis had the feeling she was tense, he said:

"Yes, let us go back, and I promise to see that you are not without a partner for the rest of the evening."

"It is very exciting to be at a Ball," Carmella said, "at the same time... I know now what it feels like to be a... 'Wallflower'!"

"Which is something you would never have been if you had a better host!" the Marquis answered.

She laughed as if he had made a joke, and said:

"No one could accuse you of being anything but a wonderful host! The trouble is... in this house there is so much to look at that I keep thinking I must see everything before I leave, for I will never have the chance again."

"I will try to prevent that from happening," the Marquis said.

"Thank you," Carmella said simply.

Then he knew that, incredible though it seemed, she had not realised there was anything personal in what he had said.

chapter six

THE Marquis kept his word and from the moment they returned to the Ball-Room Carmella did not lack partners.

Towards the end of the evening the Marquis asked her for a Waltz.

As he put his hand round her waist she felt herself quiver, and wondered why the feeling was quite different from any she had with her other partners.

Then as they swung round he said quietly:

"You dance exactly as I expected, as if you are floating on the air and your feet do not touch the ground."

"I wish that were true," Carmella answered, "but all the evening I have felt as if I were moving in a dream."

"You have enjoyed your first Ball, even though it is not a big one?" the Marquis asked.

"It is so exciting being in a beautiful room in this magnificent house, and I keep thinking that the ladies in their ball-gowns and jewels look like the swans floating over your lake."

The Marquis realised that everything to Carmella had a fairy-like quality that was unreal, and he wished he were young enough to feel like that himself.

Then as he looked down at her he said:

"Although you may not know it, Lady O'Kerry, you are a very strange person, different from anyone I have ever met before."

"I think that is only because I have always lived in a different world from yours."

"And what do you think of my world, now that you are in it?"

There was a pause, and he had the extraordinary idea that she was choosing what she should say with care rather than eulogising as most women did over the house, the parties, his guests, and of course himself.

Because she was so long in answering, he said:

"I cannot believe it has disappointed you?"

"Not your horses... nor your pictures... nor this Ball," she said quickly.

It was obvious that she was trying to avoid being rude.

She glanced at the two people dancing nearest to them. It was Daisy Brooke, looking up with rapt eyes at Lord Charles, while the expression on his face was very revealing.

Carmella did not speak but looked quickly away, and the Marquis once again could read her thoughts and knew that she was shocked.

Shocked that Daisy was married and so was Lord Charles.

Because the Marquis had moved in the Marlborough House Set for so long, he had ceased to think it extraordinary that most of the married women in it were prepared to deceive their husbands.

Or that married men, like the Prince of Wales, were continually unfaithful to their wives.

But never until now had he encountered anyone like Carmella, who was shocked by the way they behaved, even though he was aware that the Queen disapproved.

He glanced around the room at the dancers, then as

the music came to an end, Carmella said:

"I wonder if it would seem very rude if I have another look at your wonderful picture before I go to bed?"

"No, of course not," the Marquis replied, "but perhaps it would be a mistake for me to accompany you."

"You must stay here with your friends," Carmella said quickly, and he knew that, strange though it seemed, she would rather go alone.

She slipped away and a little while later the Marquis brought the evening to a close.

He knew that because his friends, especially the men, were older, they would not wish to stay up late, and there were other attractions waiting for them before the night ended.

When the Orchestra stopped playing, it was obvious that the guests from neighbouring houses were expected to say goodnight, and the gamblers at the card-tables, finding their numbers had decreased, also rose to go to bed.

There were a great many goodnights to be said, and the Marquis received effusive compliments on the success of the evening.

Then everybody was walking up the Grand Staircase, and the footmen began to dim some of the lights in the corridors.

There was no sign of Carmella, and the Marquis was certain she would have gone from the Picture Gallery to her bedroom, which was on the same floor.

She was certainly unpredictable, he thought, knowing that few women would leave a Ball-Room and their dancing-partners to contemplate a picture, however beautiful it might be.

Then, instead of climbing the stairs behind his guests, the Marquis went back to his Study to read the newspapers.

He had not had a chance to read more than the headlines during the day.

At the same time, he had another reason to be slow in going up to his room.

He was quite certain that Sybil, who was just across the corridor from him, would have left her door open, determined to make sure he did not neglect her another night.

Because he knew how determined she was to keep him in her clutches, on reaching his Study he sat down in an armchair and deliberately opened *The Times*.

His thoughts however kept returning to Carmella, and he knew, if he was honest, she fascinated him more than any woman had done for a very long time.

Because she was so youthful and unexpected, he was intrigued in a different way from any he had experienced in the past.

There was something about her, he told himself, that did not seem real: there was also something which his instinct told him was wrong.

He was not sure what it was, but it was connected with the worry in her eyes, and also her unselfconsciousness about herself.

He had never met a woman who apparently did not keep thinking of her looks and was not determined to draw attention to herself in one way or another.

"She is different, very different!" the Marquis said.

He must have sat for so long thinking about her that he dozed off without being aware of it.

Then he awoke with a start and realised it was nearly

four o'clock in the morning, and he had not been to bed.

He rose to his feet, thinking he would sleep until he was called and perhaps, as Carmella had gone to bed early, she would be riding early, as he always did.

He left the Study and walked quietly into the Hall and saw with a faint twist to his lips the night-footman was fast asleep in the padded chair where he was supposed to be on guard.

He expected that the boy, for he was little more, was tired, knowing that when he had a house-party the servants had a great deal to do.

He therefore walked up the stairs without waking him.

As he reached the landing he looked ahead and saw at the farthest end of it a figure in white and thought for a moment it might be a ghost.

Then he told himself cynically it was far more likely to be one of his guests returning to their own room.

It was unusual for it to be a woman, as it was normally the man who was expected to go back to his own bedroom.

He might have thought it was Sybil forcing herself on him because he had not been to her, if the lady in question had not already passed his bedroom, and reached the end of the corridor.

Then to his surprise he saw her turn right, where he knew there was a secondary staircase used generally only by the servants, which led down to the lower floor.

Quickening his pace, the Marquis told himself he should investigate.

Carmella, as the Marquis had anticipated, having stood for some time in front of the picture she had discovered earlier in the evening in the Picture Gallery and which she had found moved her in a strange manner, had gone to bed.

She did not want to speak to anyone, not even to Gerald.

The whole evening had been so magical that she felt as if human chatter and the problems of everyday life might spoil it.

As she got into bed she was thinking first of the picture she had just been looking at, then of the Marquis, thinking it strange that he should feel the same way as she did about it, and that it could mean so much to him.

It was not only what he said that made her aware of this, but some vibration that seemed to come from him which told her without words what he felt.

She had been aware that his voice when he spoke to her was no longer sarcastic or cynical, but deep and gentle.

It had, she thought, an undercurrent that seemed to link with exactly what she was feeling herself.

'He is very different from what I expected,' she thought.

Then she remembered how enchanting it had been to dance with him, and how, when he put his arm around her, she had felt a strange sensation within her breast that she could not explain.

Their ride yesterday morning had been wonderful.

The more she thought over what they had done and what they had said, the more she found herself seeing the Marquis's face, almost as if he were with her, and feeling that, if she could go on talking to him, he would understand.

For a moment she had forgotten about the necklace

and Gerald's debt, and she wanted to talk to him of their feelings as they had stood in front of the picture, because they seemed identical.

There were so many questions she wanted to ask him which only he could answer.

She went on thinking, and it was impossible for her thoughts to be of anything or anybody except the Marquis.

Then she heard an owl hooting far away in the distance, and realised it must be nearly dawn.

She got out of bed and went to the window to draw back the curtains and look out.

She saw there was just a faint glimmer of light in the sky behind the trees in the park, and knew it was only a question of perhaps ten minutes before the dawn would break and the stars begin to fade in the sky overhead.

It was then she knew that this was the moment when the whole house would be still and asleep, and she must go down to the safe and remove the Bramforde Necklace.

She hesitated a moment, thinking she should wake Gerald.

Then she was sure he would be deeply asleep, and perhaps, if he had drunk a great deal last night, which he might have done, he would be clumsy and even noisy and that would be dangerous.

'I will do it by myself,' Carmella thought.

Putting on the negligée which Jeanne had left for her lying on a chair, she buttoned it down the front.

It was a very pretty garment, which had been lent to her with the gowns by *Mademoiselle* Yvonne.

It was, although Carmella had not thought of it, deliberately transparent, so that the wearer's body was revealed through the thin chiffon, and the lace that trimmed it was as fine as a spider's web.

Carmella however was not thinking of herself as she impatiently pushed back her hair over her shoulders and very cautiously opened the door.

She had not forgotten that the Marquis had said there were two night-watchmen moving around the house and she could only hope that she would not encounter them.

Jeanne had told her inadvertently that there was a servants' staircase at the far end of the corridor which led not only down to the Ground Floor, but also up to the floor above, where she and the maids slept.

Because she was wearing soft, heelless slippers, Carmella's feet made no sound as she moved over the thick carpet and hurried to the end of the corridor.

The stairs were almost in darkness but she found her way down them and the floor beneath it had a light burning every twenty yards, while those in between had been extinguished.

It was not difficult for her to find her way along the passage which led to the East Wing, where the secretary's room was.

Carmella walked on cautiously, listening intently for the sound of a night-watchman.

Then as she turned the corner she saw one come out of what she knew was the secretary's room, and carrying his lantern in his hand, he walked in the opposite direction.

This meant, she knew, that she was safe for a long time.

She thought that luck was with her, but waited until he was completely out of sight before she moved slowly towards the secretary's room.

She opened the door cautiously and wondered as she did so if it would be dangerous to switch on the light.

If she did not do so, having no lantern like the night-watchman, she would be in the dark and unable to find her way.

She was just wondering whether it would be safer to pull back the curtains or raise the blind, whichever the room possessed, to let in the dawn light, when she saw to her surprise that this had already been done.

As she stared at what appeared to be an open window at the far side of the room, a shaded light went on just above the safe.

As it did so she realised with horror that she was not alone, but there was a large man standing in front of the safe, and the door of it was already open.

It flashed through her mind that it was the other night-watchman, and she wondered frantically if she would be able to retreat.

Then the man turned round and she saw to her astonishment that he was wearing a mask over his face.

For a moment Carmella and the man just stood looking at each other. Then he said in a thick, uneducated voice:

"Wot the 'ell d'yer want?"

"What are you doing here?" Carmella asked. "You are a burglar!"

In reply the man pulled a revolver from his pocket, and pointing it at her, said:

"Yer'd better be quiet, or I'll kill yer!"

Carmella gave a little gasp and he said:

"Come 'ere and sit dahn in that chair, an' don't yer

dare make no sound!"

Because she was terribly frightened and at the same time knew how helpless she was, Carmella realised the only thing she could do was to obey him.

Very slowly, aware he was still pointing the revolver at her, she came towards him and sat down in the hard chair he had pointed out that stood just in front of the safe.

"I ain't got no time to tie yer up," the man said, "but if yer knows wot's good fer yer, yer'll sit still and keep yer mouth shut 'til I've gone. D'yer understand?"

Carmella's voice seemed to have died in her throat, and she just nodded.

He stuck the revolver in the waist-band of his trousers and started to fill the sack which lay on the floor with the contents of the safe.

Carmella saw the Marquis's jewels going into it one by one, the big tiara, the necklace, the smaller tiara.

He had nearly emptied the second shelf, when the door opened and the Marquis came in.

The burglar started!

He was holding the sack in one hand and a large piece of jewellery in the other, which he had just taken from the second shelf.

He dropped both as the Marquis demanded:

"What the devil is going on here?"

Then as the burglar started to pull the revolver from his waist, Carmella realised he intended to shoot the Marquis.

Without thinking, she rose from the chair and flung herself against him just as the Marquis moved forward with the revolver pointed at him.

Small though she was, she managed to thrust the

man's arm to one side, but as she did so, he pulled the trigger.

The bullet scraped the side of the Marquis's evening-coat, while without Carmella's intervention it would have pierced his chest.

With his left arm the burglar struck at Carmella violently, and as she fell backwards her head struck the side of the iron safe and the impact caused her to scream with pain.

The Marquis caught the burglar a blow on the chin which lifted him off his feet and followed it with another which laid him prostrate on the ground, unconscious.

He then went to the side of the room where there was an alarm which rang in the servants' quarters and which he had installed for just such a situation as this.

He then picked up the revolver from the floor and put it out of reach before he bent over Carmella.

Carmella came back through clouds of darkness that seemed like a thick fog through which she could not find her way.

She thought she was lost and tried frantically to remember where she was going and why.

Then she heard voices, and as they seemed to be above her, she wondered if she had had a fall out riding.

Then because it was impossible to understand what the voices were saying and she was only aware that her whole body felt very heavy, she drifted away again into the darkness.

Carmella opened her eyes and expected to find herself in her own bed at Bramforde House.

Instead, she saw there was a canopy over her head and light coming through the curtains from the candles beside her bed.

She knew she was not at home, but somewhere else, although she could not imagine for the moment where it could be.

She tried to move, then somebody strange whom she did not know was bending over her, and a quiet voice said:

"Try to drink this, M'Lady."

There was a glass against her lips and after a moment, as the person raised her head very gently, she took a small sip, then another.

She was laid back against the pillows and the woman who seemed elderly said:

"Go to sleep. You'll feel better in the morning!"

Because it was easier to obey than to ask questions, Carmella closed her eyes.

It was morning and the light in her room now came from the sun.

As Carmella looked she knew she was at Ingleton Hall, and slowly, as if the thoughts crept into her mind rather than were there spontaneously, she remembered the sound of the revolver and the burglar's arm knocking her down.

Somebody came to the bedside and she realised it was the same woman who had given her a drink in the night.

She was wearing a Nurse's uniform.

"Are you awake, M'Lady?" she asked. "Can you understand what I'm saying to you?"

"Y-yes . . . of course."

Then with a weak little cry she asked:

"T-the . . . Marquis . . . he is all right?"

"He was not hurt, M'Lady. It was only you who fell and you've had concussion."

Carmella's eyes widened.

"Concussion? How long have I been here?"

"Two days!"

Carmella gave a little gasp.

"Now you are conscious," the Nurse said, "you'll soon get better, and I'm going to order you something nourishing to eat."

It was an hour or so later when Carmella, washed and put into a fresh nightgown, was sitting up against several pillows and asked:

"Is . . . Lord Bramforde here?"

She had almost said "my brother," then remembered.

"I'll find out," the Nurse answered, "but the Marquis asked if he could see you as soon as you were conscious."

"I . . . I would like to see him."

"I'll tell His Lordship," the Nurse replied, "but do not tire yourself. Remember, you have to rest and be very careful for a few days."

'A few days!' Carmella thought with anxiety, knowing she was still at Ingleton Hall.

She was sure the Marquis was finding her an incredible nuisance, and she wondered what had happened to Jeanne.

She was certain she must have gone back to London, otherwise *Mademoiselle* Yvonne would be very angry.

There were so many things she wanted to know; so

many questions that she felt could be answered only by Gerry; and she knew the sooner she could see him, the better.

The door opened and the Marquis came into the room.

It seemed to Carmella as if his presence filled it. She had forgotten how handsome he was, and at the same time how overpowering and yet magnetic.

He came to the side of the bed and looked down at her. Then he said:

"I have been worried in case like Sleeping Beauty you would not wake for a hundred years!"

"I . . . I am sorry to be such a . . . nuisance," Carmella apologised.

"I did not say you were that."

"But guests who . . . overstay their welcome are always . . . tiresome."

"That is something you have not done yet."

Then to Carmella's surprise the Marquis sat down on the side of the bed so that he was near to her, and said:

"I would like to start by saying 'thank you' for saving my life."

"He . . . did not . . . hurt you?"

"No, but if you had not tackled him, he would undoubtedly have shot me through the heart!"

Carmella gave a little shudder.

"Forget him!" the Marquis said. "He was a stoker of the boilers, who had been dismissed a month ago for impertinence. That is how he knew where he could enter the house and he had somehow learnt how to open a Combination safe, though I thought it was so secure."

Carmella was listening, but she did not speak, and after a moment the Marquis asked:

"How can you have been so brave as to tackle a man like that? It is difficult to know how I can thank you, but I shall be thinking about it."

He smiled at her. Then he said:

"I have had strict instructions from your Nurse that I am not to stay for more than two or three minutes, but I will come to see you again tomorrow. Then we will talk about it."

Because she thought he was leaving her, Carmella reached out her hand to take hold of his.

"Oh, please... do not leave me," she begged, "and I must know if... Gerry is still... here."

"Very much so," the Marquis answered, "and he is exercising my horses as efficiently as I do myself. I can promise you he is quite all right, and enjoying himself."

"Perhaps... I could see... him?" Carmella asked.

"Tomorrow," the Marquis answered. "You are allowed no more visitors today, so I consider myself very privileged."

He lifted her hand to his lips as he said:

"Hurry and get well. There are lots of things I want to show you."

Then before she could say any more, before she could barely realise what was happening, he had gone.

There was only the feeling of his lips, warm and insistent, on her skin.

Then as she longed to call after him and ask him to come back, she knew that, incredible though it might be, she loved him.

It was not until the next afternoon that Carmella was allowed another visitor.

The Doctor came in the morning and although he

was pleased that she was conscious and the wound at the back of her head where she had hit the edge of the safe was healing, he insisted that she must be very quiet.

"I want to see Lord Bramforde!"

Carmella knew as she spoke that what she wanted more than anything else was to see the Marquis, but the Doctor said:

"I'll tell Nurse, to allow you, unless you are over-tired, one or perhaps two visitors."

"I am better... much better!"

"Yes, I know," the Doctor said, "but you must understand, Lady O'Kerry, that we have to take every precaution with patients who have had a concussion. For far too many people do too much too soon, and have a relapse."

He was an elderly man and there was an undoubted look of admiration in his eyes as he added:

"You understand I want to be particularly careful when my patient is as beautiful as you."

"You are very kind," Carmella said, "but I must get well quickly."

"The quickest way to do that is—slowly!" The Doctor smiled.

When he left her Carmella knew that the Nurse would carry out his instructions to the letter, and there was no point in arguing about it.

She did, in fact, although she did not like to admit it, feel very limp, and she knew that to make any effort however small, would be a burden.

At the same time, she could not help worrying about staying too long at Ingleton Hall, and most of all wondering what she should say to the Marquis when he asked her why she was in the secretary's room.

It was only last night when she had lain awake for a long time in the darkness that she had known this question was bound to come sooner or later, and she had no idea how to answer it.

She could hardly say she had heard the burglar making a noise when the secretary's room was so far from her own bedroom, and from which it would have been impossible for her to hear the sound of a pistol-shot, let alone the opening of a window.

"What shall I say? What shall I say?" she asked, and wondered if perhaps Gerry had told the Marquis the truth.

Even though it terrified her to think of the questions he would ask, she wanted to see him.

She had gone to sleep feeling that his kiss was throbbing on her hand, and she could feel again the strange sensations it aroused within her.

It had been very like what she had felt when she danced with him, and yet more intense and very much more exciting.

"What I . . . feel is . . . love," she whispered.

Then she realised that she was only one of perhaps hundreds of women who loved the Marquis.

She could see the possessive expression in Lady Sybil's eyes, and the flirtatious way in which the beautiful ladies who had sat next to him at dinner had behaved, and knew she was just one of a crowd.

"It is only because I have seen so few men," Carmella argued, "and the Marquis is unique and far more outstanding than anyone I am ever likely to meet at home, or in London for that matter."

But she knew it was more than that.

It was the vibrations she felt emanating from him the moment they met, the way she could read his thoughts, as he could read hers, and the moment when they had stood in front of the picture and had both felt exactly the same about it.

"I love him, but when I leave here, I shall never see him again," she told herself, and knew that was inevitable and all the tears in the world could not change it.

Because she wanted to look pretty for the Marquis, she asked the Nurse to part her hair in the middle and brush it as it fell over her shoulders.

The Nurse was very careful because there was still a pad on the back of her head where the skin had been broken when she struck the safe, and which, when she moved quickly, gave her little stabs of pain.

She was wearing one of *Mademoiselle* Yvonne's pretty nightgowns and a dressing-jacket that went with it.

It was ornamented with rows of lace and Carmella suspected her mother would consider it far too elaborate for a young girl.

But she was not a young girl in the Marquis's eyes, she was still Lady O'Kerry, a widow, and somebody who was supposed to be sophisticated.

There was nobody to attend to her face, and she knew that the Nurse would be horrified if she asked her for the lip-salve or the rouge which she was sure were on her dressing table.

She had learned that Jeanne had left for London.

"Your lady's-maid was very sorry to go," the Nurse

had said when Carmella asked her a little hesitatingly if she was still in the house, "but she explained that her mother was ill, and she had arranged to visit her as soon as Your Ladyship left on Monday."

"Yes, of course, I remember," Carmella said quickly.

She did not ask, but she was sure that Jeanne would have taken back *Mademoiselle* Yvonne's diamonds and perhaps some of her clothes.

"Do I look ... all right?" she asked when the Nurse had finished getting her ready to see her visitors.

"You look very pretty, M'Lady," the Nurse replied, "but just remember, you're not to tire yourself, or let anything upset you."

She went from the room as she spoke, and Carmella waited.

She felt Gerald must be very anxious to see her by now, and find out exactly what had happened before the burglar knocked her down.

However, she was somehow not surprised when it was not Gerald who appeared, but the Marquis, and she saw he was wearing riding-breeches and highly polished boots.

As he took her hand in his, she asked:

"Have you been on the race-course?"

"I have," he replied, "and I left Bramforde jumping in an expert manner which I am sure would please you."

"I ... I want to see ... him."

"You can do that later, but now I want to talk to you."

Carmella stiffened and there was a wary expression in her eyes as she looked at him.

"First," the Marquis began, "I want to say how glad I

am that you are so much better and, if you are very good, the Doctor says you may get up for a little while tomorrow."

"Then we must...arrange to go...back to... London."

"Are you in such a hurry?"

"No...no...of course not, but I feel Gerald and I are...imposing on you."

There was a little twist to the Marquis's lips as he said:

"I can promise your friend Gerald is very happy. In fact, I have never known a man enjoy himself so much or find my horses far more attractive even than somebody as alluring as yourself."

"I am sure you are...very kind to him," Carmella said, "and he will be very sorry when we leave."

"I cannot understand, seeing how keen he is on riding, why he does not have horses of his own. He tells me that when he is in London he has to rely on borrowing mounts from his friends."

"He cannot afford horses."

"I thought he was well off," the Marquis replied.

Carmella did not answer.

Once again she was wondering how she could possibly explain to the Marquis that Gerry could not begin to pay his debt, and to expect him to find a thousand pounds was the same as if he asked him for the diamonds which glittered in the Ingleton tiara.

The Marquis sat down on the side of the bed as he had before, and took her hand in his.

"Now you are better," he said, "I want you to tell me why you were in the secretary's room in the middle of the night, unless you knew clairvoyantly that my life would be in danger!"

He felt Carmella's fingers tremble in his, and he said:

"I do not want you to be frightened, I want you to trust me."

Because of the gentle way in which he spoke and because the touch of his hand gave her strange sensations pulsating through her which made it impossible to think, Carmella told the truth.

"I . . . I went there . . . to . . . steal the . . . Bramforde Necklace!"

The Marquis stared at her as if he had not heard her aright. Then he said:

"To steal it? But—why?"

"We had to get it back."

"Bramforde will have it back when he pays off his gambling debt."

"I . . . I know . . . but we did not . . . want you to . . . *examine* the necklace."

"I do not understand," the Marquis said.

Carmella looked away from him, then she said:

"If I tell you the truth . . . will you swear to me . . . that you will not . . . tell anyone else?"

"Why should I?" the Marquis asked. "Of course I promise you that anything you say to me in confidence will be a secret between us."

His fingers seemed to tighten for a moment on hers, then Carmella said in a very low voice:

"The . . . the necklace is . . . false!"

"False?"

The Marquis could not help his voice sounding astonished, and it made Carmella feel that because he was shocked, it was as if he had fired a revolver at her.

'After this, he will never speak to me again,' she thought, but it was too late now to do anything about it.

She knew he was waiting for an explanation and after a moment she said in a very low, broken little voice:

"M-Mama sold the ... real stones ... so that Gerald could go to London ... and we could ... pension off the servants whom we could not ... afford to k-keep and who were too old to find other ... employment."

There was silence. Then the Marquis said:

"You said: 'Mama.' Are you telling me that—Gerald is your brother?"

"Y-yes."

Her voice was hardly audible, but now she was aware that the Marquis was staring at her, and holding her hand so tightly in his that it hurt.

"Your *brother!*" he repeated after a moment. "My darling, how could you have tortured me in this idiotic manner?"

chapter seven

CARMELLA stared at the Marquis with her eyes wide and astonished, and he said:

"I believed that Bramforde was your lover, and it has driven me nearly insane."

"My...lover?" Carmella exclaimed. "How could you...think I would do anything so...wrong or so ...wicked?"

The Marquis bent forward so that his face was very near to hers. Then he said:

"When we looked at my picture together, I wanted more than I have ever wanted anything in my life to kiss you, and now there is nothing to stop me."

As he spoke, his lips came down on hers, and Carmella knew it was not only the most wonderful thing that had ever happened to her, but what she had always longed for but thought she would never know.

Now the sensations she felt in her breast seemed to intensify.

They were so rapturous, so ecstatic, that she thought they were part of the beauty she had found in the woods at home, and everywhere at Ingleton.

She could not explain even to herself what she felt, but it was as if the Marquis's kiss came to her in music, and her whole heart was singing with the wonder of it.

He raised his head.

"It seems incredible," he said, "and yet I would

swear you had never been kissed before."

Carmella blushed.

"No...one," she murmured, "has kissed me... except you."

For a moment the Marquis just stared at her, until he was kissing her again; kissing her with long, passionate, demanding kisses, which made Carmella thrill as if he drew her heart and her soul from between her lips and made it his.

Then he said in a strange, rather unsteady voice:

"I am going to leave you, my precious, as I promised I would not make you tired, but I will come back later, and there is a great deal more I want you to tell me."

Carmella put out her hand to hold on to him, but he was already moving away, and by the time she found her voice, the door had closed behind him and she was alone.

It was then she shut her eyes and felt it could not be true that the Marquis had called her "darling" and kissed her.

She knew that her love for him had intensified until she was no longer herself, but part of him.

Nurse came back later to bring Carmella her luncheon on a tray, and after it was finished she lowered the blinds and insisted that Carmella should rest.

"The more you sleep," she said, "the quicker you will be well, and be able to go riding."

"That is what I want to do," Carmella said.

"Then you must relax," the Nurse said severely, "but just now you look a little flushed. I hope you're not developing a temperature."

Carmella knew it was because she was so excited by the Marquis's kisses, but because she could make no explanations, she merely lay quietly in the bed as the Nurse wished her to.

She shut her eyes, feeling as if the Marquis's lips were still on hers and there were thrills like shafts of sunshine running through her as she thought of him.

After a little while, she fell into a dreamless sleep and awoke to find when she looked at the clock that she had slept for nearly two hours.

The Nurse came in to draw back the curtains and she said to her as if to a child:

"You've been very good, and now there is a visitor very impatient to see you."

Carmella felt her heart give an excited leap, but when the Nurse had tidied her hair, it was Gerry who came into the room.

He was looking very smart in his new riding-clothes, and, Carmella thought, very handsome.

Yet even though she loved her brother, she knew there was no comparison between him and the Marquis.

Gerry kissed her cheek, then he asked:

"How could you have been so clever, so absolutely brilliant, as to save the Marquis's life, and of course me at the same time?"

Carmella looked at him enquiringly and he explained:

"The Marquis has just told me that he has not only cancelled my debt of a thousand pounds, but as he thinks it is unlikely our Jeweller will have sold all the sapphires we took out of the necklace, I am to ask him to return them, and the Marquis will repay the money he gave us for them, and will buy any stones which are missing."

Carmella gave a little gasp.

"Did he really say that?"

"I can hardly believe it myself," Gerry said. "But after all, you did save his life."

"Yes... I know," Carmella answered, "but how... can we take... so much from him?"

"Very easily," Gerry said, "and if he offers me a horse as well, I shall not hesitate to accept it!"

"Oh, Gerry, how can you be so... greedy when he has been so... kind!"

"I am only teasing," her brother replied, "but the Marquis has everything in the world that I would like to have."

He gave a sigh and said:

"I do not think I was ever so happy in my whole life as I have been these last few days!"

Carmella knew he was thinking of the horses and she said:

"The Marquis told me you were a very good rider, and I know Papa would have been very proud of you."

"I am proud of myself!" Gerry said. "I have never jumped such high fences before, and I suppose it is something that will never happen again."

He looked pensive for a moment, then he said:

"It is all due to you, Mella, and I think you have been wonderful! Perhaps the Marquis will ask us here another time. In fact, if he remembers that he is organising a Steeple Chase next month, I think he might invite me to ride in it."

"I hope he will," Carmella said in a low voice.

Gerry got up.

"I must leave you now," he said. "I am not going to waste a moment or do anything but ride until we actually leave."

He smiled and said:

"Do not get well too quickly! The longer you are ill, the longer I can go on riding those fantastic horses!"

Carmella laughed because she could not help it, and Gerry waved to her as he went out through the door.

She hoped the Marquis would think as she did that he was just irrepressible and not really avaricious.

She lay for perhaps five minutes before the door opened again, and now with a sudden surge of excitement like a flame running through her body she knew who had come to see her.

The Marquis had changed from his riding-clothes and was looking very smart as he walked slowly up to the side of the bed.

She looked at him, her eyes very wide with excitement, and although she was not aware of it, very revealing.

The Marquis took her hand in his and she felt a little quiver go through her.

Then as he sat down, as he always did, on the side of the bed he said:

"I suppose, Carmella Forde, you are aware that it is extremely unconventional, I might even say shocking, for me to be visiting a débutante in her bedroom!"

Carmella made a little exclamation before she said in a low voice:

"Did ... Gerry tell you that we were ... deceiving you?"

"Gerry told me it was his idea, and I think it was a clever way of bringing an accomplice to my house. At the same time, you bewildered and intrigued me from the first moment of your arrival, until I fell in love with you, and then you tortured me unbearably."

"D-did you...say that you...fell...in love... with me?" Carmella whispered.

"You know I love you!" the Marquis said. "I think we were both aware when we were in the Picture Gallery that something strange had happened to us from which it was impossible to escape."

"I think I loved you before that...but I did not... understand what I felt...because I have never been in ...love before."

"My precious darling," the Marquis said, "I cannot tell you what it means to me to know for certain what my heart told me from the moment I saw you, that you are pure and innocent, with no husband and no lover in your life."

He saw Carmella blush as he said the word "lover" and her eye-lashes were dark against the whiteness of her skin.

"If you are shocked at the idea," he remarked, "how do you think I felt?"

Because he made her feel shy, Carmella said:

"I...I want to...thank you for being so kind to Gerry. He told me what you are doing about...the necklace and that you have...cancelled the... enormous debt he...owed you."

Because she was embarrassed by his generosity, she spoke in a low voice and did not look at him.

Then the Marquis said:

"I could hardly extort such a large sum from my future brother-in-law!"

For a moment Carmella did not understand. Then she stiffened, although her fingers clung to the Marquis's.

Then she said in a small, hesitating little voice he could hardly hear:

"What . . . did you . . . s-say?"

"I was telling you," the Marquis replied firmly, "that I intend to marry you, and because, Carmella, I know that you love me, I cannot believe it is not what you want too."

Carmella looked up at him and now he could see very clearly what she was feeling.

He knew too by the way her whole body trembled that it was a shock, and yet at the same time a rapture that it was impossible to express in words.

"I love you!" the Marquis said.

Then once again his lips were on hers, and he kissed her until she felt disembodied and no longer human but part of the flowers, the sunshine, and the music that she had heard in the woods.

Then as the Marquis raised his head she said:

"I love . . . you! I love you until there is . . . nothing else but . . . love, but I know it would be . . . wrong for you to . . . marry me."

"Wrong?" the Marquis asked in surprise.

"Because . . . as you said the other night . . . I have always lived in a different world from yours . . . I would not be able to . . . make you happy."

The Marquis smiled, and there was a very tender expression in his eyes as he asked:

"Why should you say that?"

Carmella drew in her breath and he knew she was feeling for words as she said a little incoherently:

"Because our . . . worlds are so . . . different I would make mistakes . . . and I do not think your friends . . . like me."

The words were drawn slowly from between her lips and the Marquis asked softly:

"Anything else?"

"You will not . . . understand, but . . . I am . . . shocked at the way they . . . behave."

The Marquis looked down at her and thought no woman could look so lovely and at the same time so innocent and so pure.

Then he said quietly:

"I am going to tell you something, Carmella, that I have never talked about to anybody else before."

He knew she was listening as he went on:

"When I was young, younger than your brother, I fell in love with a very beautiful girl who would, from a worldly point of view, have made me an extremely suitable wife, and our marriage would have been approved of both by her parents and by mine."

He paused, then continued:

"She told me she loved me, but asked me to keep our feelings for each other secret for a little while."

The Marquis's voice hardened as he said:

"Because I was prepared to do anything she asked, I agreed, and although we saw each other almost every day and danced together at every Ball, no one was aware that we intended to be married."

As she listened, Carmella felt a wave of jealousy because the Marquis had loved somebody else.

Also he had said the girl in question was an exceedingly suitable wife for him, while she was nothing of the sort.

"Then," the Marquis went on, "just before the Season ended, when I was certain the girl I loved would allow me to approach her father and I could now tell my own parents how happy I was, she told me she was going to marry somebody else!"

Because this was not what she expected to hear, Carmella gave an exclamation of horror and murmured:

"No, oh, no! I cannot believe it!"

"I could not believe it either," the Marquis said, and now his voice was back to being cynical and contemptuous as it had been when Carmella first met him.

"My rival was a Duke," the Marquis continued, "who had inherited his title the previous year, while she knew I had to wait for mine."

He ceased speaking and Carmella asked:

"Was that the... only reason?"

"The only reason!" the Marquis repeated. "She said she still loved me, but she could not resist becoming a Duchess. Hereditary Lady-of-the-Bedchamber to Her Majesty, and to walk into dinner in front of her own mother."

"B-but how could she... think any of that... mattered?"

"It did to her," the Marquis affirmed, "but that is not the end of the story."

Carmella waited, and he said with a note of such bitterness in his voice that she could hardly bear it.

"Six years later, after she had presented her husband with an heir and also a second son, she offered to become my mistress!"

Carmella gave an exclamation of sheer horror and because she felt so shocked she would have taken her hand away from the Marquis if he had not held on to it.

"How could any... woman... behave in such a... despicable manner?" she whispered.

As the Marquis did not speak, she went on:

"But I realise... although I am very... ignorant that... that is how the ladies who are staying here for your party...behave...and that is why I could... never be the sort of wife you...want."

"The sort of wife I want," the Marquis said quietly, "is somebody who is shocked by such behaviour; somebody who would never treat me as the women we are talking about treat their husbands."

Carmella drew in her breath and he continued:

"That is why I have never married, because I have never been sure that my wife would not be unfaithful to me, not only with somebody she thought she loved, but even with the Prince of Wales, because it is the fashionable thing to do."

"B-but...it is so...wrong...so wicked!" Carmella said. "That is why...although I love you with all my heart and soul...I cannot be...your wife."

She took a deep breath before she went on:

"I want to live in the country and be happy as Papa and Mama were happy...and have...children who would not be ashamed of their mother...or their father."

She spoke for the moment as if she were not shy, but with a conviction that was too strong to be denied.

Then because she was afraid the Marquis would be angry, she said in a faltering little voice:

"I...I am sorry...I am sorry...if I hurt you... but I cannot...pretend...and I know if you ever behaved...like Lord Charles and...all those other men...I would want to...die!"

The Marquis was silent for a moment, then because his feelings were overwhelming he said:

"My darling, my precious, innocent little love! Do you think I want you to feel any other way? You are what I have always been looking for, but thought I would never find. How can I be so marvellously lucky, not only to find you and to love you, but to know that you love me?"

He bent forward and put his hands very gently on each side of her face, then said:

"Look at me, Carmella, look at me!"

She obeyed him and he saw the worry in her eyes and also that she was not far from tears.

"Listen to me, my lovely one," he said, "I swear, because I love you as I have never loved anyone in my whole life, that I will be faithful to you! We can forget what goes on in London and what happens in what is known as 'The Marlborough House Set,' because we shall be living here, here at Ingleton or in one of my other houses in the country, with our horses and, please God, in the future, our children."

"Do you... mean that?" Carmella asked. "Do you really... mean it?"

"I mean it," the Marquis said, "and I swear before God that I will make you happy!"

Then he was kissing her, and somehow it seemed to Carmella he was kissing her now in a different way.

Although his kisses were possessive and demanding, there was also something reverent in them, as if she were infinitely precious and, although it seemed a strange word, he respected her.

"I love you... I love... you!" she said when he set her free.

Then she looked up at him a little tremulously as she added:

"I can... really marry you?"

"Do you think I could lose you now?" the Marquis asked. "We are going to be married very soon, and very quietly, my darling, and I think, as Gerald tells me your mother is not well, it is an excellent excuse for us to be married here and tell everybody about it afterwards."

"You mean... we shall not have to... ask all your ... friends?"

"We will be married in the Chapel here," the Marquis said, "and we will have with us only the people we love, who will understand that the 'Fashionable World' is no longer my world and instead I am moving into yours."

Carmella gave a laugh of sheer happiness.

Then after the Marquis had kissed her until she was breathless he said:

"All you have to do is to get well quickly, and leave me to arrange everything."

"I love you!" Carmella murmured because there were no other words to express what she was feelling.

The Marquis and Marchioness of Ingleton drove away in a Chaise drawn by four superlative horses, and as they did so Carmella asked:

"Am I really... your wife? I still find it... hard to believe."

"I will make you sure of it tonight," the Marquis promised, and turned his head from his horses to watch his wife blush, and thought it made her even more beautiful than she was already.

To Carmella, it seemed unbelievable that everything had happened so quickly.

She had left everything to the Marquis, as he had told her to do, and she had known, because she was learning to be very perceptive about him, that he enjoyed organising her life in the same way as he organised the perfection of his own.

He had refused to allow her to return to London, but sent for Lady Bramforde, who was so excited at the news that her daughter was to marry anybody so important and at the same time so charming as the Marquis that she had seemed to get well as quickly as Carmella did.

Gerald was in his element because he could spend more time with the horses.

The day before their marriage the Marquis said to Carmella:

"I have just arranged something which I think will please both you and your mother."

"What is that?" Carmella asked.

"That Gerald should go into my old Regiment—the Life Guards."

Carmella looked astonished and the Marquis said:

"I think it would be a mistake for him to waste his time in London, where he may once again gamble away money he has not got. We really cannot keep restoring the Bramforde necklace to its original perfection!"

He was teasing and Carmella said:

"We are so ... grateful for ... all you have done for us, and now you are thinking of Gerald ... and trying to keep him out of ... mischief."

She was to find later that the Marquis had given Gerald an allowance to match that of most Officers in the Life Guards, and he had also sent his Estate Manager and other members of his staff to Bramforde House to see what could be done about it and the estate.

Last night, before they went to bed, when they dined

quietly in the small Dining-Room, the Marquis had said:

"I think I may have some news for you, Gerald, at the end of the week."

"News?" Gerald questioned.

"I have heard that a very rich American, whom I know slightly, is looking for a house he can rent for about five years in a hunting area. But because he is not a particularly social person, he does not want to be among the smart set in Leicestershire."

Carmella's eyes lit up and she replied:

"Do you mean he might take Bramforde?"

"I have told him about it, and he says it seems ideal. Moreover, being exceedingly wealthy, he is prepared to spend a large sum of money in making the house comfortable, which I can tell you will include not only renovating the rooms and practically refurnishing them, but also, because he is an American, installing bathrooms."

Gerald gave a cry of excitement and Carmella said:

"Does that mean he will also pay rent?"

"A very large one, if Maynard has anything to do with it," the Marquis said, "and I think that with any luck, by the time the estates have been put in order and made a paying concern under a competent Manager, when Gerald has finished being a soldier, he will be able to retire to being a country gentleman, as I intend to be myself!"

It was impossible for Gerald or Lady Bramforde to thank the Marquis enough, and he was obviously embarrassed by their gratitude.

When he was alone with Carmella before she went to bed she asked:

"How can you be so marvellously kind and generous to Gerry? If he is happy, so is Mama. And I do not think it is possible for me to be any happier than I am at this moment."

"I intend that you shall be very much happier when you are my wife," the Marquis said.

"It is ... difficult to tell you how ... grateful I am."

"It is the only way I can show you how grateful I am for being alive," the Marquis said, "for if you had not saved me, Carmella, I would not be here to tell you how much I love you, and how I am longing for the night to pass so that tomorrow you will be mine."

Then as she wanted to go on thanking him he kissed her and it was impossible for her to think of anything but that she loved him to distraction.

The Chapel, which had been built at the same time as the house, was very beautiful.

It was massed with white flowers, especially lilies, and the fragrance of them, the soft music coming from the organ, and the atmosphere of sanctity made Carmella feel as if she had stepped into a special Heaven and that everything from now on, because she had the blessing of God, was Divine.

The Marquis's gift of a wedding-gown which had come to her from London was exquisite, as was the trousseau he had ordered for her.

She knew when she looked at them that only somebody with not only an artistic sense, but an acute sensitivity where she was concerned would have been aware of exactly what suited her.

She told the Marquis a little shyly how she had borrowed her clothes from Gerald's friend *Mademoiselle* Yvonne, and although he had laughed, he said:

"That is something you will never have to do again,

and although I will tell Gerald to give *Mademoiselle* when he sees her a very appropriate present from us both, I shall make sure, my darling, that the Yvonnes of this world will not encroach upon the quiet life we shall be living in the country."

"Our new world!" Carmella said softly.

"A world of love," the Marquis replied, "and that, my precious, is what you have brought me and which I will never lose."

Now, driving away from Ingleton Hall, Carmella asked as they turned out of the drive:

"You have not told me yet where we are going."

"It is a secret," the Marquis replied, "because I want us to be entirely alone, with no visitors, no distractions, until we come back home, where there will be a million things for us to do. First of all, although I have not told you about it until now, the whole Estate will want to celebrate our marriage."

Carmella looked at him wide-eyed and he said:

"That means they will eat and drink a lot and roast a whole ox, and of course they will expect fireworks."

"Which I shall enjoy as much as they will," Carmella exclaimed. "I have seen fireworks only once in my life and I thought they were very exciting."

"Then we will have a very splendid display," the Marquis promised. "My darling, there are so many things you have never had before that I want to give you, and to share with you."

He saw Carmella smile and instinctively he drove his horses a little faster as if he was eager to reach their destination.

They reached it in under two hours and Carmella found that it was a charming house built in the style of an Italian Villa with gardens sloping down to the River Thames.

"I bought the house a long time ago," the Marquis said, "when I was interested in learning to paddle a canoe. Now I will be able to take you on the water, if you wish."

He smiled before he added:

"But I think we shall be happy in the garden, which was made by one of my relatives into one of the most exotic and beautiful gardens in the whole country."

Carmella found this was true.

The house was exquisitely furnished and very comfortable, in fact a luxurious dolls'-house version of Ingleton Hall.

She knew as there was beauty all around them that it was just the place she would choose for a honeymoon with the man she loved.

Later that night in a room fragrant with flowers and in a large bed draped from a corolla in the same way that *Mademoiselle* Yvonne's had been, but very much more tasteful, Carmella looked round her.

The room was filled with antique furniture so that each piece was a part of history and the pictures were all by famous artists.

They made her feel she was riding on the clouds which would carry her into the world of love that the Marquis had promised her.

When he came into the room, he pulled back the curtains so that they could see the evening stars coming out one by one in a translucent sky.

Then he walked to the bedside to say as he looked at her:

"How can you be so lovely?"

"I want... you to think... so."

"You are mine," the Marquis said softly. "All of you, from the top of your head to the soles of your little feet. I have never ever owned anything so precious."

"Suppose... I turn out to be... a fake like the... sapphires?"

The Marquis laughed.

"I knew that what you pretended to be was not genuine, and that you were very different from what you appeared to be. I could not be deceived."

"I... would never do... anything to hurt you... because you are so... wonderful and I love... you."

There was a note in Carmella's voice which put the fire into the Marquis's eyes. He got into bed and took her into his arms.

"I have dreamt of this," he said, "and now, my adorable little wife, I want to teach you about love. It will be the most exciting thing I have ever done in my whole life."

"Teach me... oh, teach me... how to make you... happy," Carmella begged, "and to be... exactly as you want me... to be."

Much later the stars were like diamonds glittering against the sable of the night, and the moonbeams coming in through the open windows turned everything to silver.

Because she was so ecstatically happy, Carmella moved nearer to the Marquis and whispered:

"How can I... tell you how much I... love you?"

He drew her closer as he said:

"You have told me that already, my precious one, and I only pray I have not hurt you in any way."

"I... I did not know that... love could be so wonderful... so marvellous!"

"What did you feel?"

He thought, as her body quivered against his and she felt for words, that he had never known such happiness existed.

"I... felt as I did when we... looked at your beautiful picture," Carmella said, "as if... the stars and the flowers were... part of our love. Then you carried me into the sky... and there were little... shafts of moonlight moving through me... which made it impossible to think... but only to... feel. It was... perfect and very beautiful... but also very exciting!"

"I did not frighten you?" the Marquis asked.

"You know you did not," Carmella answered, "but I did not... realise... I did not... know that love was like... fire."

She thought the Marquis was questioning what she said and explained:

"First there was the... moonlight inside me... then it seemed to turn to little flames... and I could feel them flickering... and I thought... perhaps you felt ... the same."

"I felt a fire that has consumed me ever since I first met you," the Marquis said. "A fire, my precious, that is not just passion, but which purifies and burns away all that is evil and wrong, and leaves only what you and I are both seeking; all that is pure and good."

Because she was surprised that he should speak in

such a way, she looked up at him in the moonlight and said:

"How can you say all the things I want you to? I never thought that any man would... think the same way as... I do."

"We think the same, we feel the same, we are the same!" the Marquis answered. "We are one person, my lovely one. Just as I am part of you, so you are part of me, and we cannot be divided."

"That is what I want," Carmella cried, "now and for ever! I am yours, completely yours... please... love me... and never leave me... because I could not... lose you."

"You will never do that," the Marquis said in a deep voice, "and I believe our love will deepen, and, although it seems impossible, grow greater year by year."

He kissed her very gently as he said:

"I love and worship you!"

Carmella instinctively moved closer to him.

As he felt her heart beating against his, his lips, from being gentle and very tender, became more insistent.

He went on kissing her, his hand touching her body, and Carmella could feel the moonlight moving within her.

Once again it was changing from the beauty of its silver light into little dancing flames.

They were leaping within her breast until, as they reached her lips, they met the fire burning within the Marquis.

Then as everything that was beautiful around them seemed to intensify, and as their need of each other was irresistible, the Marquis carried Carmella up into the sky.

As he made her his, they found the perfection of love which everybody seeks, but which in its purity and beauty, is the world of God.

ABOUT THE AUTHOR

Barbara Cartland, the world's most famous romantic novelist, who is also an historian, playwright, lecturer, political speaker and television personality, has now written over 430 books and sold over 400 million books the world over.

She has also had many historical works published and has written four autobiographies as well as the biographies of her mother and that of her brother, Ronald Cartland, who was the first Member of Parliament to be killed in the last war. This book has a preface by Sir Winston Churchill and has just been republished with an introduction by Sir Arthur Bryant.

Love at the Helm, a novel written with the help and inspiration of the late Admiral of the Fleet, the Earl Mountbatten of Burma, is being sold for the Mountbatten Memorial Trust.

Miss Cartland in 1978 sang an Album of Love Songs with the Royal Philharmonic Orchestra.

In 1976 by writing twenty-one books, she broke the world record and has continued for the following eight years with twenty-four, twenty, twenty-three, twenty-four, twenty-four, twenty-five, twenty-three, and twenty-six. She is in the *Guinness Book of Records* as the best-selling author in the world.

She is unique in that she was one and two in the

Dalton List of Best Sellers, and one week had four books in the top twenty.

In private life Barbara Cartland, who is a Dame of the Order of St. John of Jerusalem, Chairman of the St. John Council in Hertfordshire and Deputy President of the St. John Ambulance Brigade, has also fought for better conditions and salaries for Midwives and Nurses.

Barbara Cartland is deeply interested in Vitamin Therapy and is President of the British National Association for Health. Her book *The Magic of Honey* has sold throughout the world and is translated into many languages. Her designs "Decorating with Love" are being sold all over the U.S.A., and the National Home Fashions League named her in 1981, "Woman of Achievement."

In 1984 she received at Kennedy Airport America's Bishop Wright Air Industry Award for her contribution to the development of aviation; in 1931 she and two R.A.F. Officers thought of, and carried, the first aeroplane-towed glider air-mail.

Barbara Cartland's Romances (a book of cartoons) has been published in Great Britain and the U.S.A., as well as a cookery book, *The Romance of Food*, and *Getting Older, Growing Younger*. She has recently written a children's pop-up picture book, entitled *Princess to the Rescue*.

BARBARA CARTLAND

Called after her own
beloved Camfield Place,
each Camfield novel of love
by Barbara Cartland
is a thrilling, never-before published
love story by the greatest romance
writer of all time.

March '87...DANCING ON A RAINBOW
April '87...LOVE JOINS THE CLANS
May '87...AN ANGEL RUNS AWAY